Tow-Truck
Pluck

Annie M.G. Schmidt
& Fiep Westendorp

Tow-Truck
Pluck

Translated by David Colmer

PUSHKIN CHILDREN'S BOOKS

Pushkin Children's Books
71–75 Shelton Street,
London WC2H 9JQ

Original text © 1971 by the Estate of Annie M.G. Schmidt,
Amsterdam, Em. Querido's Kinderboeken Uitgeverij

Copyright illustrations © 1971, 1982, 1983 Fiep Amsterdam bv;
Fiep Westendorp Illustrations

English translation © David Colmer, 2011

Tow-Truck Pluck first published in Dutch as
Pluk van de Petteflet in 1971

This translation first published by Querido's Kinderboeken
Uitgeverij in 2011

This edition first published by Pushkin Children's Books in 2016

10 9 8 7 6 5 3 2 1

ISBN 978 1 782691 12 9

Cover Brigitte Slangen

Cover illustration Fiep Westendorp

Inside Design Irma Hornman, Studio Cursief

Printed in China by Imago

www.pushkinchildrens.com

Contents

Pluck Finds a Home

Pluck had a little red tow truck. He drove it all over town looking for somewhere to live. Now and then he stopped. And when he stopped, he asked people, 'Do you know anywhere I can live?' The people thought for a moment and then said, 'No.' Because all the houses were taken.

In the end Pluck drove into the park. He backed his truck in between two trees and sat down on a bench.

'Maybe I can sleep here in the park tonight,' he said out loud. 'I could sleep in my truck under that tree...' Then he heard a voice above him. 'I know where you can live,' the voice said.

Pluck looked up. There was a beautiful, fat pigeon sitting on one of the branches of the big oak tree.

'The tower of the Pill Building's free,' the pigeon said.

'Thanks,' Pluck said, taking off his cap. 'Where is the Pill Building? And what's your name?'

'I'm Dolly,' the pigeon said. 'And the Pill Building's close by. That great big building over there... See? Right up on top, there's a little tower. And in that tower, there's a room. And no one lives in it. If you're fast, you can move into that room. But don't waste any time, otherwise it might be taken.'

'Thanks,' said Pluck, and he hopped into his tow truck and drove to the Pill Building. He parked out the front, went in through the glass doors and stepped into the lift.

Whooshhhhh, up he went.

When the doors opened again, he was outside at the very top of the building. His hair was blowing in the wind, and it was so high up it scared him and made him feel dizzy. But there was Dolly the pigeon on the railing. She had flown up to the top, faster than the lift, and now she was sitting there waiting for him.

'Come on,' she said. 'That's right. Follow the walkway. Look, there's the door to the tower. It isn't locked. You can move right in.'

Pluck went inside. The room inside the tower was fantastic. It was round and it had lots of windows. Because it was so high up, you could look out over the whole city. There was a bed and a chair and a wardrobe, and there was a sink.

'Do you think I can move in here just like that?' Pluck asked.

'Of course you can,' Dolly said. 'It's empty, isn't it? Have fun in your new room and I'll see you later. I'll come and visit.' And Dolly the pigeon flew off, back to the park.

Pluck was very happy to have a place of his own. He stayed there for a whole hour looking out at the view, constantly changing windows and constantly seeing different parts of town. Until he got hungry.

'I'll go do some shopping,' he said. 'On the ground floor of this building there's a whole row of shops. I noticed them on the way in.'

He took the lift back down. But this time there was someone else in it too. It was a lady with a big spray can in one hand. She looked

7

Pluck up and down. And then she asked, 'Do you live here?'

'Yes, ma'am,' said Pluck politely.

'Where?' the lady asked. 'Which flat? Which number?'

'I live in the tower,' Pluck said.

'The tower?' the lady asked. 'You don't say!' She looked at him again with very cold eyes and Pluck was afraid that she was about to ask 'Do you have permission?' or 'Have you rented it?' But fortunately, the lift arrived downstairs before she had time to ask him anything else, and Pluck hurried out, running through the glass doors to the row of shops. He bought a loaf of bread and some milk and a bag of apples.

'I think that's all I need,' Pluck said. 'Oh no, that's right. I wanted to get a really good comic to read.'

He went into the bookshop. A friendly old man was standing behind the counter. And while Pluck was looking through the comics, the old man asked, 'Do you live here in the building?'

'I live in the tower,' Pluck said. 'I just moved in.'

'Lucky you,' the old man said. 'Have you met anyone else who lives here yet?'

'No,' Pluck said. 'At least... Oh, that's right. There was a lady in the lift with a spray can.'

'Heavens above! With a spray can? That must have been Mrs Brightner. Where was she going?'

'I don't know,' Pluck said. 'She was in the lift and she went all the way down, just like me. Except I think she kept on going... Is that possible? To the basement or something?'

'Oh yes, definitely! Listen, son,' the old man said, 'I'm Mr Penn. What's your name?'

'Pluck.'

'Good. Look, Pluck, would you please go down to the basement? It's the first green door in the lobby and then down the stairs.'

'What do you want me to do there?' Pluck asked.

'It's like this,' Mr Penn said, 'that Mrs Brightner walks around all day spraying everything that moves with that can of hers. All over the place. That can is for flies and mosquitoes and moths and so on... Do you know what I mean? But the basement is where Zaza lives.'

'Who's Zaza?' Pluck asked.

'A friend of mine,' Mr Penn said. 'Zaza is a cockroach.'

'A cockr –' Pluck blurted in surprise, but Mr Penn gave him a shove and called out, 'Quickly, please! Hurry... otherwise she'll spray Zaza dead.' Pluck raced out of the shop, into the hall, through the green door and downstairs to the basement, where a nasty smell met him. The smell of a spray can.

He was in a very large room. It was hot and dry: there was a big boiler for the central heating and apart from that it was empty and gloomy and echoing and full of the horrible smell of spray can.

The first thing Pluck did was open a window. Then he went looking for Mr Penn's friend. A cockroach... *Who on earth makes friends with a cockroach?* thought Pluck. And he called out, 'Zaza!'

There was no answer. One step at a time, Pluck covered the whole basement, searching everywhere until he finally saw something lying in a corner. An insect. It was Zaza the cockroach. He was lying on his back with his legs in the air. Dead.

'Poor Zaza,' Pluck said. He picked up the cockroach and laid it close to the open basement window. Then he went back to Mr Penn.

'Too late,' Pluck said. 'He's dead.'

Mr Penn sighed. 'It's not that I'm crazy about cockroaches in general,' he said. 'But you see, this was a very special cockroach, a very friendly cockroach, and so intelligent. Dead, you say? From that spray can, of course. One day Mrs Brightner will kill off every living thing around here with that spray of hers. She's always running around with that spray can. When she's not scrubbing or sweeping, at least. She's too clean, you see. And too tidy. Things never shine bright enough for her, she always has to brighten everything up... I think that's how she got her name. But thanks for trying, son, and drop by again sometime.'

Pluck went back to the lift with his shopping, but suddenly realized that he'd left the bag of apples in the basement. He hurried back down the stairs to get them. Just as he was about to leave again with the apples, he heard a quiet, bashful little voice saying, 'I wouldn't mind a piece of apple peel.' Pluck turned around in surprise. There, close to the basement window, stood Zaza the cockroach, a picture of health with all six feet firmly on the ground.

'I fainted,' he said. 'But I'm better now. Will she be back with that terrible spray?'

'I don't know,' Pluck said. 'But I think you'd be better off up in my tower with me. She doesn't go there. And from now on you can have all my apple peelings.'

Carefully he picked Zaza up and put him in the bag with the apples.

When he went to bed that night, he was very happy. *I have a place to live*, he thought. *And I've already got two friends. No, three. Dolly and Mr Penn and Zaza.* 'Are you comfy in there, Zaza?' he called out.

Zaza was lying in a matchbox lined with cotton wool. 'I'm fine!' he shouted in his tiny little cockroach voice.

'See you in the morning then,' Pluck said. And he fell asleep.

The Stampers

You couldn't imagine a more beautiful room in the whole world than Pluck's little room at the very top of the Pill Building.

In the morning when he got up, the first thing he did was look out through all the windows. He saw the whole city, he saw the sky and the clouds, he saw the traffic down below him and, if he leant out of the window far enough, he could even see his own little tow truck parked downstairs on the pavement.

When he was ready for breakfast he called out to Zaza first to wake him up. He was really a very nice and very polite cockroach. He lived off apple peel and hardly ate any of that either, so he wasn't an expensive houseguest.

After a few days in the Pill Building, Pluck had got to know a few more people. He knew the doctor and old Mrs Jeffrey, and he also knew the big ginger tom, the Pill Cat, but Pluck didn't get on very well with him, because he stalked birds. He even stalked Dolly, who sometimes came to sit on the walkway outside Pluck's room. The Pill Building was enormous and very tall. There were more than twenty floors and sometimes Pluck took the lift from one floor to another. He'd walk along the walkways and look at all the doors to see who lived in the different flats. Sometimes he'd stop to talk with someone and almost everyone was nice to him.

One morning, he saw a little boy sitting on the tiled floor near the lift. He was holding a bottle and crying. Pluck stopped and wondered what had happened.

The boy looked up with a tear-stained face and said, 'Sir, do you know where I live?'

'Don't you know how to get back home?'

'No. Do you know where I live, sir?'

'Just call me Pluck,' Pluck said. 'I'm no sir. What's your name?'

'I'm a Stamper,' the little boy said. 'I'm one of the little Stampers.'

'What do you mean? Is that your name?'

'Yes.'

'I think...' Pluck thought deeply for a moment. He'd seen the name Stamper on the front door of one of the flats. 'Come with me. I think you're on the twentieth floor. I'll take you back home.'

He took the boy into the lift and on the way up he asked, 'You've got brothers, haven't you?'

'Yes,' the boy said. 'There's six of us. Six little Stampers and one dad. And my five brothers have all got measles. But not me. That's why I had to go to the chemist. To get some medicine.' He held up the bottle.

The lift stopped at the twentieth floor and when the little boy looked out, he shouted happily, 'Now I remember! This is our walkway!'

'Remember, it's the twentieth,' Pluck said. 'Then you can't go wrong.'

'I live here,' the little boy said. The door to the flat opened and Mr Stamper was standing there in an apron with an enormous spoon in one hand. 'At last,' he exclaimed, 'you're back.'

'I got lost,' said the little Stamper.

'And I showed him the way,' said Pluck.

'Come in,' said Mr Stamper. 'Come in. I've seen you around. You're the one with the tow truck, aren't you? Who lives up in the tower? I'm just frying up some chips. Never mind the smoke. Ignore the mess. Come in. Then you can have some chips.'

'Oh, no,' Pluck said, 'there's no need for that.' But Mr Stamper pulled him in, shouting, 'Don't be silly! The best chips in town! Never mind the mess.'

It really was a terrible mess inside the flat. There were jumpers and trousers and comics everywhere. And the floor was covered with mattresses. Sewn-together mattresses lying wall to wall. It was nice and soft to walk on, but your shoes sank into it and Pluck stared at it with surprise.

'That's for the noise,' Mr Stamper explained. 'We have Mrs Brightner living right below us. Do you know her?'

'I've seen her around sometimes,' Pluck said.

'Well, you see, Mrs Brightner kept complaining about the noise because of all the little Stampers stamping on the floor so much, you see? And this is what I came up with. The best thing is that we don't need chairs anymore. We all sit on the floor. But we've got beds to sleep in. See.'

Pluck looked up. There were seven bunks against the wall. One for Dad and six for the boys. And there were sick Stampers lying in five of the bunks. They didn't look sick at all and they climbed out of bed. They were cheerful, messy little boys with amazingly bushy hair.

'Are you Pluck?' they cried. 'Pluck with the tow truck? Pluck with the cockroach? How's the cockroach?'

How did they know all these things? Pluck blushed. He hadn't known there were people in the building who already knew him. He asked, 'Who told you that?'

'We saw the tow truck!' the Stampers cried. 'And Mr Penn told us that you rescued Zaza the cockroach.'

'And you've got a pigeon too, haven't you?' screamed the smallest Stamper. 'The big fat one? Dolly?'

'She's not *my* pigeon,' Pluck said. 'She's a

free pigeon from the park. She's just a friend of mine.'

Now Mr Stamper appeared with an enormous bowl full of chips. They all sat down on the mattresses on the floor and started eating chips with mayonnaise and ketchup. They spilt a lot on the mattresses but that didn't bother the Stampers at all.

'Oh no...' Mr Stamper said suddenly, 'we're such idiots!'

'Why? What's the matter?'

'We invited Pluck in. And now he might get measles... and it will be our fault.'

'No,' Pluck said. 'I've already had measles. You can't get them twice.'

When the chips were finished, Mr Stamper said, 'Have you met Aggie yet?'

'No,' Pluck said. 'Who's Aggie?'

'A little girl in a pink dress. A pink dress that's always perfectly neat and tidy.'

'Oh, yeah,' Pluck said. 'I saw her out on one of the walkways the other day. I think she was bored. I asked her if she wanted to come and play but she didn't want to.'

'She's not allowed to...' Mr Stamper said, 'the poor girl.'

'She's not allowed to play?' Pluck asked.

'She's not allowed to get dirty,' said Mr Stamper. 'Aggie is Mrs Brightner's daughter and she's never allowed to play outside because her mother's scared she'll get dirty.'

'But that's horrible!'

'It is. And that's why... if you see her again... you should try to get her to go with you, so she can play and have fun for once. Out on the street or in the park.'

'I will,' Pluck said. 'And thanks for the chips... Bye. Does Aggie live right under here?'

'Yes!' shouted the little Stampers. 'Right under here. And when we make a racket, her mum gets really angry.'

Pluck said goodbye, promising to come back soon. He took the stairs down to the nineteenth floor and saw her standing there, the little girl called Aggie. She was leaning over the rail and staring into the distance. Her dress was very pink and very pretty and very clean. But her face looked sad and Pluck decided to talk to her. He coughed shyly. He wasn't sure how to start, but just then he heard wings flapping. Dolly the pigeon flew up and landed on Pluck's shoulder.

'Pluck, you have to come straightaway. You have to help. Hurry...'

Dizzy

'What is it?' Pluck asked.

'It's an emergency!' Dolly exclaimed. 'Someone's in danger!'

'Who?'

'Quick...' Dolly cried again, fluttering around nervously. She called out, 'Third oak on the left... near the pond.' And then she flew off.

Pluck wanted to go straight to the lift. He started running, hoping to get to the park as fast as he could, but after two steps he stopped and turned back. The girl in pink was still standing there next to the railing. Mrs Brightner's daughter: immaculate Aggie. She was never allowed out because she always had to stay clean. Pluck stepped towards her and said, 'Listen, would you like to help me?'

Aggie looked up in surprise. She had been leaning over the rail staring out at the view the whole time and hadn't even noticed Pluck and Dolly's conversation.

'I have to go to the park with my tow truck,' Pluck blurted. 'I need to rescue someone.'

'You need to rescue someone?' Aggie said. 'Who? How?'

'I don't know yet,' Pluck said. 'But I'm worried I won't be able to manage it alone. Will you come with me, please?'

Aggie hesitated. Then she shook her head. 'I'm not allowed,' she said. 'I'd get dirty in the park. That's what my mother says. I'm not allowed to go to the park, ever.'

'You are if it's to rescue someone,' Pluck said. 'You coming? Or not? There's no time to waste.'

Aggie shook her head. 'I'd get in trouble,' she said.

'Fine,' said Pluck. 'I'll go alone.' And he hurried off to the lift. But just before the door shut, Aggie ran up, panting. 'I'll come after all,' she said.

A little later they were on their way in the red tow truck. Pluck drove as fast as he could and Aggie trembled and held on to the seat, calling out, 'I won't get dirty, will I? I'm sure my mother won't approve. I don't even know who you are! Or what your name is!'

'I'm Pluck. And you're Aggie. So stop whining,' Pluck snapped. 'Here's the park. The pond is just around this corner. And now it's the third oak on the left.'

'That must be this one,' Aggie said. 'This is the third oak on the left. What's supposed to be happening?'

Pluck had stopped his truck. Together they stared up. But they couldn't see anything.

'What are we looking for?' Aggie asked.

'Someone in danger,' Pluck said.

'I can't see anyone in danger,' Aggie said. 'No one *in* danger and no one *out of* danger, if you see what I mean... I can't see anything at all. Except for a squirrel.' She pointed. 'You see that squirrel? Right up at the top?'

'Yes,' Pluck said. 'But I can't see anything special about it.'

Nearby the leaves rustled. It was Dolly sitting on a branch. 'So you made it at last,'

she said. 'Did you see him? The poor thing?'

'What poor thing?' Pluck asked. 'All we can see is a squirrel.'

'That's him!' Dolly cried. 'That's Dizzy. A very sad case. He's scared of heights.'

'Scared of heights?' Pluck asked. 'A squirrel who's scared of heights?'

'Yes, tragic, isn't it? It's very rare in squirrels. He's too scared to climb. Ever. Well, you can imagine how the rest of the family makes fun of him. That's why he tried it for once. Now he's right at the top... but he's too scared to come back down. So help him, Pluck. With your crane!'

Pluck drove his truck as close to the tree as he could get it and raised the crane until it was just below the branch the poor animal was sitting on. But it didn't reach up high enough. There was still quite a gap. Dizzy would have to jump. But Dizzy was scared of heights and hung on tight.

'Come on, Dizzy, jump! Jump onto the crane.'

Nothing happened. The poor animal was petrified.

'I'll get him,' Aggie said.

'You sure?' Pluck asked. 'What about your dress? What about your mother?'

But Aggie had forgotten all about her dress and her mother. She was already halfway up. She climbed smoothly from branch to branch and in no time she was close to the frightened squirrel. She reached out to him, but he crept back fearfully.

'Stay still, silly!' Aggie cried. 'I almost had you.' She climbed after him, reached out... and grabbed him.

'Hold on to the crane!' Pluck shouted. 'Then I'll lower you down.'

Aggie held on to the crane and soon she was safe in the truck with Pluck, holding the squirrel in her arms.

'What do we do with Dizzy now?' Pluck asked. 'Does he have to stay on the ground?'

'No!' Dolly cried. 'No! That's much too dangerous. He'd get eaten by a cat or a rat.'

'Then we'll take him with us,' said Pluck, who turned to Aggie and got the shock of his life. She looked terrible. It wasn't just that her dress was covered with green and brown smudges. It was also torn from climbing through the branches. She noticed it too and got very frightened.

'Pluck...' she said quietly, 'I'm scared. I can't go home like this.'

Pluck thought for a moment. 'We'll go see Mr Penn,' he said. 'Maybe he's got an idea.'

They drove back to the Pill Building and Pluck stopped at the bookshop.

'We've got a squirrel who's scared of heights...' Pluck said as they walked in, 'and Aggie's dirty and messed up and too scared to go home.'

'Tell me more,' said Mr Penn. Pluck told him the whole story and finished by asking, 'Shall I take Dizzy up to my tower with me?'

Mr Penn shook his head. 'A tower is the last place to put a squirrel who's scared of heights,' he said. 'I've got a better idea. He can learn how to climb in my storeroom. Come with me.'

At the back of the shop there was a room where Mr Penn kept his supplies in tall cupboards and bookcases. There were ladders all over the place for him to get to the top shelves. Mr Penn put the squirrel on the bottom rung of a ladder. 'So,' he said. 'Now you can get some practice, Dizzy. When you feel like it. Move up one rung at a time, then you'll get used to it.'

They went back to the shop, where Mr Penn shook his head as he looked at poor, dishevelled Aggie. 'Hmm...' he said. 'What are we going to do about this?'

'I'll never be able to go home again....' Aggie moaned.

'Nonsense,' said Mr Penn. And suddenly he clicked his fingers and cried, 'I know! We've got Keep-em-on Cleaner's right next door.'

'What's that?' Pluck asked.

'Come and see,' said Mr Penn. 'It's a laundry service where you don't have to take off your clothes. They wash them while you're still wearing them. That's why it's called Keep-em-on Cleaner's!' Mr Penn took them next door and said a few words to the lady from the laundry.

'Just pop into the steam booth for a minute, dear,' the lady said. She opened a kind of wardrobe and pushed Aggie in. Then she pressed a button. There was a buzzing noise on the inside and wisps of steam came out through the chinks.

'Isn't it dangerous?' Pluck asked anxiously. 'All that steam... Can she breathe in there?'

'Don't worry,' the lady said, 'we do this all the time.' She opened the door to let Aggie out. She was perfectly pink, without a stain in sight. But her dress was still just as ripped.

Aggie was about to start moaning again about being too scared to go home, when the lady from the laundry grabbed her arm and said, 'Now just step up onto the spraying disc.' She put Aggie in the middle of a big disc and pressed another button. The disk rotated while a gigantic spray can began to spray. Aggie turned around and around as a pink fluid sprayed out over her.

'It's a kind of plastic,' said Mr Penn, who was also watching. 'Once it's dried, all the rips and tears will be fixed.'

The lady turned off the machine. After spinning around so much, Aggie was as dizzy as Dizzy and Pluck had to grab hold of her.

'Careful...' the lady said, 'she's still wet. You have to give it a minute to dry.'

It was incredible. There wasn't the slightest trace of a rip. They had all been filled with spray. Aggie was spotless again and in one piece. Pluck reached out to touch her. 'She's dry!' he shouted.

'Lovely,' said Mr Penn. He paid the lady and said, 'Go home anytime you like, Aggie. You're totally respectable!'

'Can we have a quick look at Dizzy first?' Pluck asked.

'Let's.'

They went back to Mr Penn's storeroom, opened the door a crack and peeked in. Dizzy was sitting on the seventh rung of the ladder.

He had a brave look in his beady little eyes and was about to jump over to another ladder. Silently and with bated breath, they stood there watching.

Jump! He did it.

'See... he's making progress,' Mr Penn said. 'So, bye for now.'

Pluck went into the Pill Building lift with Aggie.

'Thanks for helping me,' he said. 'Would you like to come out again sometime?'

'I'd love to,' said Aggie.

Longmount and the Major

Behind the Pill Building there was a small park on the bank of a wide canal. One morning Pluck drove past it in his tow truck. Then he stopped. There was something weird in the water. He could see it sticking up above the surface... It was brown... It had a tail... Oh no, it was a horse's bottom!

'A drowned horse...' Pluck mumbled, shaken. 'That's terrible.' He got out and walked over to the waterside. Yes, now he could see it very clearly. It was the rear end of a horse. And the head was nowhere in sight.

'The poor thing,' Pluck said. 'Its head must be stuck in the mud.' He looked around for someone to help, but there was no one else in the park. Then he saw something else sticking up out of the water a bit further along.

Pluck walked up to it. To his astonishment it was another horse. But this time it was a horse's head!

'Two horses in the canal!' Pluck exclaimed.

'No,' the head answered. 'Just one.'

'One?' Pluck cried. 'That's not true... There's two of you! I just saw another horse over there.'

'That's me too,' the horse moaned. 'That's my bottom.'

'But... that's impossible,' Pluck sputtered.

'I'll wave my tail,' the horse said. 'Then you'll see.'

Pluck saw the tail swishing back and forth in the distance.

'You... you must be a very long horse.'

'I am. I'm Longmount, the world's longest horse.'

'Where do you live? And who's your owner? Who looks after you?' Pluck asked.

'Why don't you just help me up onto the bank?' Longmount said. 'Lend a hand, instead of standing around for hours nagging and asking questions. Is that a tow truck you've got there or what?'

'I'm sorry,' Pluck said. 'Of course I'll help. Do you think you could come a bit closer to the bank?'

Longmount struggled over to the side of the canal. Pluck attached the hook of the tow truck to the horse's halter and climbed into the cab. 'Ready now... Here we go!' he shouted.

Just then two men in army uniforms came running round the corner. 'Longmount!' they shouted. 'What happened?'

'He fell into the water,' Pluck said. 'I'm trying to pull him out.'

'That shows a lot of gumption, my boy,' said one of the men. 'I'm the Major and this chap here is my adjutant. Longmount is my horse. Reel him in!' Pluck started his engine and bit by bit the horse came up out of the water.

'You have to help too!' Pluck yelled.

'I'm trying!' Longmount shouted. 'My hooves are stuck in the mud.'

'How could you be so careless?' the Major asked. 'I've warned you so many times.' And to Pluck he said, 'If I'm not mistaken, you're the young fellow who lives in the tower? I've seen you round. I live in the Pill Building too, you know. Do you like it up there?'

'Oh yes,' Pluck said. 'It's a great place to live.'

'Are you going to stand there all day?' Longmount snorted. 'I'm getting colder and colder. Hurry up, will you?'

It took a very long time, but in the end all four of the horse's legs were up on dry land.

'Thank you, thank you...' said the Major, 'and if I can ever help you with anything... it will be my pleasure! You never know, maybe I can do something in return one day. Cheerio.'

'Bye,' said Pluck.

The Major climbed up onto Longmount just behind his head. The adjutant climbed on too, but near the tail. 'We always ride him like this,' the Major explained. 'Longmount is afraid that otherwise he'll sag... He never lets anyone sit in the middle.'

Longmount trotted off and Pluck watched them go. It was only two people on one horse, but it looked like a whole procession.

Pluck still had some shopping to do. He arrived back home loaded down with bread and pears.

'Zaza!' he called. 'Zaza, where are you? Zaza, do you like pear peel too?' He couldn't see the cockroach anywhere.

Pluck searched and searched, and was starting to get worried. Then finally he heard Zaza's tiny little voice, 'Careful! Don't stand on me!'

Pluck looked down at his feet. 'Where are you?'

'Under the mat,' the little voice said.

Carefully, Pluck raised the mat and, sure enough, there was Zaza.

'What are you doing there? Were you hiding?'

'That lady came back,' Zaza said. 'The lady with the spray can.'

'What? Mrs Brightner? Did she come in?' Pluck asked. 'She can't have, I always lock the door. And I take the key with me.'

'She didn't come in. She looked in through the window,' Zaza said. 'And she saw me. I was terrified. I thought she was going to spray me through the window. That's why I ran away to hide.'

'She's gone now,' Pluck said. 'Come on out.'

He gave the poor frightened cockroach a piece of pear peel, but after tasting it, Zaza said, 'No, apple peel's better.'

'OK,' Pluck said. 'It was worth a try.'

But that same afternoon, when he was on

his way out, a man came up to him in the lobby of the Pill Building. A man in a peaked cap. It was the Pill Building doorman and he looked very unfriendly.

'Tell me, sonny,' he said. 'Is it true you're living upstairs in the tower?'

'Yes,' said Pluck. 'I live there.'

'Since when?' the doorman asked.

'Er... since about a week ago...' Pluck mumbled.

'And who gave you permission?' the doorman asked.

Pluck hesitated for a moment. Then he said, 'Nobody...'

'Just as I thought,' the doorman said. 'You sneaked in! Without a rental agreement or anything. And you didn't even ask me first!'

Now he looked even less friendly.

'Why didn't you ask me?' he demanded.

Pluck was about to say, 'I didn't even know you existed.' But he held his tongue instead, because it didn't seem like a very good answer.

'I wouldn't have even known,' the doorman said, 'if Mrs Brightner hadn't told me. And it's a good thing she did. Little boys who move into houses without telling anyone are up to no good. So pack your things and get out of that tower, understood?'

Pluck stood there listening with a bright red face. He felt tears welling up. He had found a home, and a lovely home too, and now he had to move out. He sniffed and wiped the tears from his cheek with the back of his hand.

'What's going on here?'

Standing next to him was the Major. He had taken Longmount to pasture and now he was on his way back to his flat. 'What's the problem?' he asked again.

'This young man has moved into the tower,' the doorman said. 'And he doesn't have a lease or anything. He has to go!'

'Stuff and nonsense!' said the Major. 'No one was living in that tower. That room has been empty for ages. You should be glad to have someone living there. And such a nice

boy too, who helps everyone with his tow truck.'

'But –' the doorman began.

'No buts…' the Major snapped. 'I say he stays. And no more complaining. Understood?'

'Yes, Major, sir,' the doorman said.

'So, that's settled then. Cheerio, my boy.' And the Major hurried off to the lift.

The doorman sighed. 'All right then,' he said, 'we'll leave things as they are for now.'

'I can stay?' Pluck asked.

'For now…' the doorman said.

Relieved, Pluck went out through the glass doors of the Pill Building. He hadn't noticed that Mrs Brightner was in the lobby too. She had heard the whole conversation between Pluck, the Major and the doorman. And now that Pluck was gone, she came out from her corner. She went up to the doorman and whispered something.

'What?' the doorman said. 'Can't you speak up a little?' Mrs Brightner spoke up a little. And the doorman's face went as white as a sheet.

Zaza

Two hours later Pluck came home. He went upstairs with the lift and walked to his tower room. When he got close to the door he smelt something peculiar... Some kind of floor cleaner? It was a strange smell... Some kind of wax?

No! Pluck froze with horror. It was spray! He could smell the fumes from a spray can. He fumbled for his key and tried to open the door, but he couldn't. His key didn't fit anymore. Only then did he see the sign:

MRS BRIGHTNER'S
SEWING ROOM

Pluck was furious. In the time he'd been away, Mrs Brightner had stolen his room. Even though she already had a flat of her own!

He pounded on the door. Nothing happened. He pounded even harder. The door opened halfway and Mrs Brightner's head appeared.

'What do you want?' she asked.

'I live here!' Pluck cried. 'What are you doing in my room?'

Mrs Brightner looked him over from top to toe and then said, 'I shall tell you exactly what I am doing. You don't live here anymore. It is now my sewing room. Ask the Pill Building doorman.'

'That can't be right! It's not fair!' Pluck shouted. 'I've always lived here!'

'*Lived* here, yes...' Mrs Brightner smiled. 'But a boy who doesn't keep his room clean has to go. That's obvious. And the doorman agreed.'

'I did keep my room clean,' Pluck screamed.

'Really?' Mrs Brightner asked. 'You think so? A room where cockroaches just walk around freely, is that what you call clean?'

'What have you done with my cockroach?' Pluck asked fearfully.

'I'll tell you what I've done with it,' Mrs Brightner said. 'I saw it sitting in a corner and I gave it a good spray with my spray can. Then I threw it in the rubbish bin. Out there. Next to you.'

Pluck jerked the lid off the rubbish bin. It was empty. 'The garbage men were just here,' Mrs Brightner smirked. 'You can still hear them banging around downstairs. But there's no point searching, you know, the filthy beast is dead.'

And she banged the door shut in Pluck's face.

Pluck wasn't the kind of boy who cried easily. In fact he never cried at all, but now he felt a strange lump in his throat and tears started to run down his cheeks. His little friend Zaza was dead. And he'd lost his room. Then he heard wings flapping next to him. It was Dolly the pigeon.

'Coo-coo... coo...' she said. 'You needn't say a word about it, I saw it all. I was right here! I saw that Mrs Brightner go inside with the doorman. She complained and said it was crawling with cockroaches! And then she got them to put in a new lock. And she's got the key. Don't just stand here crying. Go see Mr Penn instead. He always knows what to do. You take the lift, I'll fly down. We'll see each other in a minute.' And Dolly flew off.

When Pluck got down to street level, he saw the garbage truck still standing there. Two men were busy emptying rubbish bins into the truck and when they saw him, they called out, 'Hey, Pluck!'

Pluck almost asked, 'Have you seen a dead cockroach perhaps?' But he held back.

Garbage men don't pay any attention to dead cockroaches and besides... what good would it do? Zaza was dead anyway. There was nothing anyone could do about it. Pluck called out hello and went to Mr Penn's shop.

'There you are again at last,' Mr Penn said. 'How are you? Look at this wonderful picture I've got. With astronauts in it.'

'Nice...' said Pluck in a high, squeaky voice.

'What's wrong? You're crying! What's happened?'

Pluck told him what had happened, then laid his head on the counter and sobbed, 'I liked Zaza so-so-so-so much!'

Mr Penn put the picture down and paced back and forth furiously. 'Stealing your room!' he cried. 'Outrageous! But we won't take this lying down. We'll do something about it, my boy, you can count on that.' Someone tapped on the shop's glass door. It was Dolly.

As soon as Mr Penn opened up, she flew in. She was holding something in her beak. Something black. Very carefully, she laid it on the counter.

'Zaza!' Pluck screamed. 'Oh... poor Zaza. Dead... but now I can at least give him a proper burial.'

'Thank goodness for that,' Mr Penn said. 'But wait a minute... is he dead? Isn't he wriggling his legs?'

Zaza was lying on his back. And it was really true. If you looked closely, you could see his legs moving slightly.

Mr Penn fanned him with a sheet of paper, then turned him over onto his feet. Zaza stayed standing. For a long time they stared at him intensely. Then Zaza said in a very tiny, very weak voice, 'Am I still alive?'

'You certainly are,' Mr Penn said.

'Has that horrible pigeon gone?' Zaza asked.

'Well, I never!' Dolly cried indignantly. 'Did you hear that? After I saved his life. Fishing him out of the garbage truck. I flew past and I saw him lying there. And now he calls me a horrible pigeon!'

'Shhh...' Mr Penn said. 'He doesn't mean it.'

'And I was so proud of myself for not eating him!' Dolly exclaimed.

Pluck had picked up Zaza and was looking at him tenderly. 'Are you feeling any better?' he asked.

'I'm fine,' Zaza said.

'Watch what you're doing!' Mr Penn shouted angrily at Dolly. 'Right on my beautiful, expensive picture of astronauts.'

'Sorry,' Dolly said. 'It's because I'm excited. But you can wipe it off again. It's not dirty. It's all mine.'

'Ugh!' Mr Penn grumbled as he tried to scrape the mess off with a piece of paper. But the picture was ruined.

'I'm putting you outside,' Mr Penn said.

'Don't be ridiculous,' Dolly said. 'If I've just been, I won't have to go again anytime soon, will I?'

'Control yourself then. And let's start talking about Pluck's room. In any case, you can stay here, Pluck. I'll set up a camp bed for you in the storeroom. And Zaza can have a little box to sleep in.'

'First I want some apple peel,' said Zaza.

And they gave him some.

Carl with the Wooden Leg

Pluck no longer had a home. The round room in the tower wasn't his anymore. Now there was a sign on the door saying: MRS BRIGHT-NER'S SEWING ROOM. And Mrs Brightner went there to sew every day from nine to five. There was a new lock on the door. And she had the key...

Pluck was staying at Mr Penn's. He slept on a camp bed in the storeroom behind the shop. Next to him, in an empty drawing-pin box, slept Zaza, who had fortunately made a full recovery. It was quite cosy really, but Pluck still longed for his own little home.

In the morning, when he got up, Mr Penn said, 'Let's go and talk to the Pill Building doorman first. He's given your room to Mrs Brightner. He got a new lock put in with a new key. Come on!'

The Pill Building doorman was sitting in the glass booth in the downstairs lobby. When he saw Mr Penn and Pluck coming towards him, he jumped. His face turned red and he started acting like he was extremely busy.

'Doorman,' said Mr Penn. 'This is our Pluck. You know him very well. He lives upstairs in the tower. You know that, don't you? And now you've taken his room away from him!'

The doorman cleared his throat self-importantly and said, 'Yes! It can't be helped. Sorry!'

'Can't be helped!' exclaimed Mr Penn. 'You have to throw Mrs Brightner out. She's already got her own flat. She can sew there as much as she likes.'

'Listen here,' the doorman said. 'There were complaints. That boy didn't keep his room clean. It was crawling with cockroaches. I saw it myself.'

'Just one!' Pluck cried indignantly. 'There was only one cockroach!'

'See, he admits it!' the doorman said. 'He admits that there were cockroaches?'

'One cockroach,' Pluck said. 'One very special, very friendly, tame cockroach!'

'Now, look here,' said the doorman. 'Under no circumstances are cockroaches allowed in the Pill Building. That's obvious, surely? What if everyone kept one friendly tame cockroach as a pet? What would that lead to? Next year we'd have twenty thousand cockroaches in the building. They breed like flies!'

'You're exaggerating,' Mr Penn cried angrily. 'You know very well that one little insect won't hurt anyone. I'm going to complain to THE BOARD about this!'

'You do that...' the doorman said, 'it won't help you one little bit. The board will only tell you that cockroaches are not allowed. It says so in THE REGULATIONS!'

'Please, just give –' Pluck began, but the phone rang and the doorman sat down to answer it without giving them a second glance.

They realised it was pointless even talking to him and trudged back to the bookshop.

Dolly the pigeon was standing on the pavement.

'And? How did it go?' she asked.

'Badly,' Mr Penn replied. 'He won't even listen to us.'

'If only I could help,' Dolly said. 'I know... every time Mrs Brightner comes out of the tower, I'll do something.'

'What will you do?' Pluck asked.

'I'll do something on her head!' Dolly cried. 'I'll do something on her dress!'

'It's sweet of you to come up with a plan,' Mr Penn said. 'But I'm afraid she'd just ignore it. She'd just put up an umbrella or something like that... Plus I think it's a horribly dirty idea.' And Mr Penn went into his shop, because he had work to do. Pluck stayed out on the pavement for a moment talking to Dolly.

'I've got another idea!' Dolly cried. 'Wait here... I'll be right back.'

Pluck waited patiently. After about seven minutes, the pigeon came flying up again.

'I asked him to help...' she said. 'But he's so gruff and superior... It would be better if you talked to him yourself.'

'Who?' Pluck asked.

'Carl! Come with me. He's on that pole over there!' Dolly flew off and Pluck ran after her.

Perched on top of a traffic sign was an enormous seagull. Like most seagulls, he had bad-tempered eyes and a dissatisfied look on his face.

'This is Pluck,' Dolly said.

The seagull screeched and gave a little hop. 'I know you!' he cried. 'Just the other day you gave me a sardine!'

Then Pluck saw that the seagull had a wooden leg.

'It was delicious,' Carl said. 'I'll see what I can do for you. I hear they stole your room in your tower! We can do something about that!'

'That would be fantastic,' Pluck said. 'Have you already got an idea... um... sir?'

'Call me Carl!' the seagull with the wooden leg screeched. 'It's like this, I've got six brothers. And lots of cousins. I tell you what... leave it to me. It might take a day. It might take longer. You'll see!' And with a mighty whoosh of his wings, the seagull flew off.

'Ship ahoy!' he called out as he went, because he was a real seagoing seagull.

It was now nine o'clock in the morning. Mrs Brightner took the lift up to the top floor of the Pill Building. She was in a good mood because she had a beautiful piece of material in her bag. She was going to make herself a dress. A dress with flowers on it. Singing quietly to herself, she followed the open walkway to the tower. A big screeching seagull flew past, just over her head. Mrs Brightner didn't pay any attention. She was thinking about her new dress.

When she had reached the tower and was about to unlock the door with her key, a second seagull skimmed past her head.

'Seagulls...' she muttered. 'Nasty creatures...' She went inside and locked the door. Her sewing machine was on the table. She took the things out of her bag and set to work. The room in the tower had windows in all directions.

And soon seagulls arrived. They couldn't get in, they just flew past. At first it was only two. Then more showed up.

With shrill cries they flew at the windows as if they were planning to smash right through them, then turned away at the last moment. Their wings beat against the glass with a horrific sound.

Now there were so many seagulls that when Mrs Brightner looked out, all she could see was their wild white fluttering... Furious eyes glared in at her and the shrieks grew deafening.

'Go away!' Mrs Brightner yelled. 'What

do you want anyway? Nasty creatures!'

She poked her tongue out at the seagulls. She called them names and waved her arms to chase them away, but it was no use. More and more arrived... and they kept flying around the tower. They pecked at the windows with their beaks and their screeching began to sound so menacing that Mrs Brightner got frightened.

'You can't get me anyway!' she called. 'I'm nice and safe inside! And you can't get in! Stupid seagulls!'

No, it was true, they couldn't get in. She was safe inside. But sooner or later she'd have to go back out... This afternoon at five o'clock... then she'd have to go back to her own flat... she'd have to open the door... and then she'd have to walk down that long walk-way... What if they were still there? Mrs Brightner was scared.

She'd lost her interest in the floral dress she was sewing. She waited for the seagulls to go away. But they didn't go away. And this was just the beginning...

The Seagulls

Mrs Brightner sat at her sewing machine in the room in the tower. With deafening shrieks, the seagulls flew past her windows. How many were there?

There's at least a hundred, thought Mrs Brightner. *I don't dare to go outside... but I have to, because I forgot the blue silk thread. I have to go back to my flat to get it. I'll just have to be brave... they're only birds, after all. They can't hurt me... I'll take the spray can.*

Bravely she stepped out of the door and onto the walkway.

Umph! With a fearful screeching, the seagulls swooped down on her.

'Help! Go away! Nasty creatures!' Mrs Brightner yelled. She sprayed all around with her spray can, but seagulls aren't scared of spray cans. She lashed out, swinging her arms wildly, and dropping her bag in the process. Spools of thread and packets of needles scattered all over the walkway.

'Monsters!' Mrs Brightner screamed. Struggling hard, she fought her way forward step by step. An enormous tangle of fluttering seagulls blocked her path. They didn't hurt her, they didn't peck her, they just touched her now and then with their wings, that was all. But their screeches were so menacing and they glared at her so furiously, landing on her and brushing past her face... Mrs Brightner was exhausted by the time she reached the lift and could go down to her flat to get the silk thread.

When she arrived back at the top floor, she was wearing a kind of armour. A colander on her head, an enormous plastic raincoat and a big flag to ward off the birds.

But the moment she stepped through the glass doors and onto the top walkway... terrible... it was like a blizzard darkening the sky... the seagulls flew past right in front of her, they landed on the floor, they flapped in

front of her eyes, they screeched horrifically! Mrs Brightner couldn't take another step. She turned back in fury and took the lift down to the lobby to see the doorman.

The doorman seemed a little surprised by the strange apparition with the colander on her head and a big flag in one hand.

'What's happening?' he asked.

'Could you please come with me for a moment...' Mrs Brightner panted. 'I have a seagull problem.'

'A seagull problem?' asked the doorman. 'What kind of a problem?'

'They're attacking!' Mrs Brightner cried. 'Millions of them!'

'I'll come with you,' the doorman said.

They went upstairs in the lift and looked out at the walkway through the glass doors. The doorman said, 'Where are the seagulls?'

There wasn't a seagull in sight.

'Come outside,' Mrs Brightner said. 'They'll come once we're on the walkway.'

But even when they were outside on the walkway, nothing happened. It was a bit windy, but otherwise totally quiet and peaceful.

'They're gone!' Mrs Brightner cried. 'Gone forever! How wonderful!'

'I can go then, can I?' the doorman asked.

'Yes, certainly, and thank you very much!' Mrs Brightner said cheerfully.

But the moment the doorman went down in the lift... Oh, no! The whole pack of seagulls swooped down out of the sky.

'Help!' Mrs Brightner screamed. 'Murder! Fire!' She took three desperate steps towards the tower, then fled head over heels back to the safety of the lift.

On the way down, at the thirteenth floor, someone else got in. It was the Major.

'Good gracious, Mrs Brightner,' he said. 'Is something wrong? Just look at you!'

She really did look terrible. The colander was crooked on her head. Her raincoat was in tatters and so was the big flag.

'Oh, Major,' she said. 'What a stroke of luck bumping into you. May I borrow your gun for a moment?'

'My gun? Why? Has the enemy breached your defences?' the Major asked.

'No... yes...' cried Mrs Brightner. 'I'm being attacked by gulls –'

'What?' interrupted the Major. 'An attack of gallstones, you say? My rifle's no good to you then.'

'Gulls! Seagulls!' Mrs Brightner yelled. 'Murdering gulls! Please come upstairs with me. You'll see.'

'With pleasure!' the Major said. But when they reached the top floor, there wasn't a seagull in sight.

'See? It was all a dream,' the Major said.

'No, it wasn't! I wasn't dreaming. They only come when I'm alone!'

'But what are you doing up here anyway?' the Major asked. 'You live much lower down. You don't need to be here at all.'

Mrs Brightner swallowed. She didn't dare admit that she had stolen Pluck's tower and was using it as a sewing room. The Major said a polite goodbye and went downstairs. And

no sooner was he gone then... There they were again... mobs and hordes of screeching, fluttering seagulls. The biggest one of all had a wooden leg. He beat his wing against Mrs Brightner's arm, making her drop the key. The key to the tower.

Immediately another seagull swooped down, snatched up the key and flew off with it.

'Give that key here!' Mrs Brightner tried to barge past the wings but there were too many. She had to give up.

Pluck was sitting on the bookshop step. He didn't know anything about what was happening and felt miserable because he'd lost his home and hadn't heard anything from Carl the seagull... who was supposed to be helping him.

And then something fell with a clink on the ground in front of his feet. It was the key to his tower.

He looked up and saw an enormous seagull flying off with slow steady flaps of its wings.

A little later Mrs Brightner came up to the doorman and said, 'I've had enough!'

'You've had enough of what?' the doorman asked.

'I've had enough of that horrible tower,' Mrs Brightner said. 'It's a pirate's nest! It's a gruesome, grisly murderer's den! Please be so kind as to fetch my sewing machine away from there as soon as possible!'

'Of course, Mrs Brightner.'

When the doorman arrived upstairs at the tower ten minutes later, the sewing machine was already out on the walkway along with a few other things. Pluck was standing at the door... trembling slightly. Would the doorman throw him out again?

'Hmmm...' the doorman said. 'You're back in your room, I see.'

'Yes,' said Pluck. 'I'm back in my own room. And you can take Mrs Brightner's things with you if you like.'

'So... I hope you're going to keep your room clean from now on,' the doorman said sternly.

'Oh, yes, I'll make sure of it,' said Pluck.

'Remember, no more filthy creatures!' the doorman said. 'You don't have any filthy creatures in there, do you?'

'No,' Pluck said, 'no filthy creatures.' He wasn't fibbing. Because although Zaza the cockroach was inside in the cupboard, he wasn't a filthy creature. He was just good old Zaza.

'OK, then,' the doorman said. He picked up the sewing machine and the other things and took them downstairs.

Dolly the pigeon flew up and landed on Pluck's shoulder.

'They did it!' she cooed. 'The seagulls chased her off! Congratulations, Pluck!'

'Thanks,' said Pluck.

'Put three locks on your door this time,' Dolly said. 'You never know!'

'I'll do that,' Pluck said. 'Have you seen Carl with the wooden leg anywhere? I want to thank him.'

'They're gone,' Dolly said. 'All the seagulls have gone to the harbour. A boatload of fish just arrived.'

'I'll see him sometime,' Pluck said. And then he went inside. He was very happy!

The Airlift

Pluck was living in his tower again. He had his home back and he could look out over the park and the city. And he was chatting to Dolly the pigeon, who was sitting on his window ledge.

'Hey, Dolly,' Pluck said, 'have you seen Aggie lately? I haven't seen her anywhere.'

'Aggie? She's probably home. Go and visit!'

'It's too scary,' Pluck said. 'If I went to visit I'd have to ring the doorbell. And then her mother might answer. And her mother's Mrs Brightner! I'm too scared of her!'

'I've got an idea,' Dolly said. 'She lives on the nineteenth floor, doesn't she? I'll go and have a look. I'll fly past the window. I'll be right back.'

Dolly flew off. And a few minutes later, when she came back, she called out 'Sick!' while she was still in the distance.

'Is Aggie sick? Tell me about it... Was she in bed?'

Dolly landed back on the window ledge and said, 'Well, there's a balcony next to her bedroom, see? So I sat on the rail of that balcony and I was able to look in. And she's lying in bed. And everything's pink. Her pillow is pink and the rug on the floor is pink and –'

'Yeah, yeah,' Pluck blurted. 'Everything's pink. Get to the point!'

'The doctor was there,' Dolly said. 'He wasn't pink. He was about to give her an injection.'

'Poor Aggie,' said Pluck. 'If only I could drop in on her. But I'm too scared... You know what? I'll write her a letter. Will you deliver it for me?'

'Deliver a letter!' Dolly yelled excitedly. 'May I? Oh, how fabulous, then I'll be a real carrier pigeon! That's just what I've always wanted!'

'That's right,' Pluck said, 'then you'll be a carrier pigeon.' He wrote a letter. This is what it said:

Dear Aggie,
It's horrible that you're sick. Get better soon.
Bye,
Pluck

'And put it in a real envelope,' Dolly said. 'With a real stamp on it!'

'No, no stamp,' said Pluck. 'You don't need stamps with carrier pigeons.'

He licked the envelope and stuck it down and said, 'Here, take it. Be careful! And only give it to her if she's alone in the room.'

'Of course,' Dolly said. 'What do you take me for? I'm not silly.'

She flew off with the letter. It seemed to take a very long time for her to come back. Pluck waited anxiously... What was keeping her?

Ahhhh... finally... there she was. With a letter in her beak. A pink letter.

'Did she write back?' Pluck called. 'Here, quick, give it to me.'

He opened the letter. And this is what it said:

Dear Pluck,
I've got measles and I'm dying for a piece of
liquorice, but I'm not allowed to eat sweets in bed
because my mother says it's dirty.
Bye,
Aggie

'She wants some liquorice,' Pluck said.
'Maybe you can take her some. I've got a
whole roll here.'

Dolly tried to pick up the roll of liquorice,
but it was a little too thick for her beak.

'Wait, I've got a better idea,' Pluck said. He
got out a small basket that had once con-
tained mini-Easter eggs and put a few pieces
of liquorice in it with a few fruit gums. 'Can
you manage this? Try it.'

'Easy,' said Dolly.

She picked up the basket and flew off. Aggie
always kept her balcony door open and Dolly
could fly straight in. But first she landed on the
balcony rail and peeped in carefully. Aggie
was alone. She was very happy with the sweets
and gave the empty basket back to Dolly.

This was the start of a kind of airlift between Pluck and Aggie. They sent letters to each other and every day he sent her a basket of sweets.

It went well for three days. But on the fourth day Aggie fell asleep with a piece of liquorice in her mouth. And when Mrs Brightner came to check on her, there was a black stain on the pillowcase. 'Liquorice!' her mother shouted. 'Where did you get that liquorice? Filthy child! I absolutely forbid it!'

'Yes, Mummy,' Aggie said. But that day Dolly came again.

Her mother's bedroom was next to Aggie's. And her mother's balcony was next to Aggie's balcony. And between the two balconies there was a planter box with plants in it. When Dolly arrived, Mrs Brightner was standing on her own balcony, hidden behind the plants. She saw Dolly fly into Aggie's room.

Now I know how that child gets that filthy liquorice, she thought. *That filthy seagull brings it.* (Since the day the seagulls had chased her off, Mrs Brightner thought of all birds as seagulls.)

'I'll put a spanner in those works...' she muttered.

'Hey, Dolly...' Aggie whispered. 'I'd really love an ice cream... Could you manage that?'

'I'll see...' said Dolly, who passed the message on to Pluck. And the next day she brought a beautiful pink ice cream in her basket.

But it was quite heavy. And because of that, Dolly fluttered a little lower than usual and a little slower than usual... She was trying hard to get there as fast as possible, because the ice cream was starting to melt... And because of that she wasn't very alert... Poor Dolly!

She didn't know that Mrs Brightner was on the other balcony. And she didn't see the terrible creature leering at her. It was the doorman's enormous, big, fat ginger tom. Normally he lived downstairs in the lobby, but Mrs Brightner had lugged him upstairs and now she was holding him under one arm. And just when the pigeon was coming in to land with the heavy basket, Mrs Brightner pushed the cat through the plants and let him drop on Aggie's balcony.

Dolly got a terrible fright. She immediately tried to fly up, but the ice cream was too heavy... and the cat was about to leap up at her...

Dolly let go of the basket.

And *floop!* The ice cream fell on the Pill Cat's head.

The cat sat there with a big lump of pink ice cream on his head. The ice cream ran down into his eyes. He couldn't see a thing for a moment and let out a long pathetic meow.

Mrs Brightner looked on. 'Stupid cat!' she cried. 'Idiot! Now the seagull's got away!' In all the confusion, she hadn't seen Dolly fly in through the door. She didn't know that Dolly

was now fluttering around Aggie's room.

'There's a cat on the balcony...' Dolly cried fearfully.

Aggie got out of bed. She closed the balcony door and said, 'Come here, I'll hide you... in my chest of drawers!'

Dolly in Danger

Aggie lay there in her pink bed. The balcony door was shut and outside the Pill Cat was licking ice cream off his face. Dolly the pigeon was in one of Aggie's pink drawers.

The bedroom door opened and Mrs Brightner came in with a cup of soup on a tray.

'I saw a seagull fly in with that filthy liquorice,' she said. 'That's why I brought the Pill Cat up here to chase it away. To make sure it doesn't happen again.'

'Yes, Mum,' said Aggie.

'Here's your soup,' said Mrs Brightner. 'That's better for you than all those disgusting

sweets. And we'll leave the Pill Cat on the balcony for the time being. To make sure that seagull doesn't come back. Here, take the soup. Then I'll get your bib out of the drawer.'

'No!' Aggie screamed. Only now did she realise that the bib was in the drawer she'd hidden Dolly in.

'What do you mean?' Mrs Brightner asked. 'You have to put a bib on!'

'I mean... I... I haven't got a spoon...' Aggie spluttered. 'There's no spoon to eat the soup.'

'I'm sure I put a spoon on the tray. Huh, you're right. I'll just go get one.'

Mrs Brightner went to the kitchen to get a spoon. And quick as lightning, Aggie jumped out of bed and pulled open the drawer.

'Let me out onto the balcony...' Dolly said.

'No! The cat's out there...' Aggie whispered. 'Quick... under the bed.'

Just in time, Dolly disappeared under Aggie's bed. Mrs Brightner came back with a spoon. And a broom. 'Here,' she said. 'And now I'll sweep under the bed.'

'No!' Aggie cried again.

'Stop making such a fuss about everything,' her mother said. 'I have to keep things clean!'

'I'll get dust in my soup!' Aggie cried.

'No, you won't... What nonsense. I'll open the balcony door so it can blow out!'

'No! Don't open the balcony door! The cat will come in!'

'You're not scared of a cat, are you?'

'Yes, I am,' Aggie said. 'The cat's covered in ice cream. I'll get ice cream all over my rug... and then...'

'Fine. I'll sweep with the door shut.'

Aggie held her breath... She'd run out of ideas... Her mother grabbed the broom and... *Trrring!* It was the doorbell!

'Someone's at the door!' cried Aggie.

'I'm on my way,' her mother said. She leant the broom against the wall and went into the hall.

'Where do I go now?' Dolly asked from under the bed.

'Into the wardrobe,' Aggie said. 'Wait, I'll open the door...'

But it was too late. The doctor came in and Dolly only just managed to sneak back under the bed in time. Aggie jumped back into bed.

'Here we are again!' the doctor exclaimed. 'How is the young lady today? A little better, I see! You're already eating soup. But turn over onto your tummy first. For your injection!'

Meekly, Aggie turned over onto her stomach. She wasn't scared of injections because they didn't hurt at all. But she was very scared of her mother finding Dolly. Soon, when the doctor was gone, her mother would start sweeping and then she'd discover the pigeon under the bed.

'There,' the doctor said after he'd given her the injection. 'I'll put a little plaster on that. You're a very brave girl. And you'll be better in no time. Tomorrow you can get up and play for a while.'

'Would you like some soup too, doctor?' Mrs Brightner asked. 'Or would you prefer a cup of coffee.'

'Oh, no, thank you,' the doctor said. 'I'm in much too much of a hurry. I can't stay.'

'I'll show you out,' said Mrs Brightner.

'No need. I can show myself out. Oh, yes, there is one other thing. As soon as she's better, she should go to the seaside for a while. That would do her the world of good. Bye!' He took his hat and left.

'To the seaside...' Mrs Brightner said. 'Then I'd have to go to the seaside with you? But I couldn't possibly. I don't like the seaside. Seagulls everywhere! Ugh... Now, what was I about to do? Oh, that's right, sweep!'

'Not under the bed!' Aggie cried.

'What's got into you?' her mother asked. 'Why not under the bed? You're not hiding something under your bed, are you? You naughty girl!'

She bent down and looked under the bed. Aggie groaned softly and hid her head under her pink pillow.

'Nothing,' she heard her mother say. 'For a moment there I thought you had a whole supply of filthy liquorice under your bed. But there's nothing at all.' And with a powerful thrust, she pushed the head of the broom under the bed.

Aggie came back out from under the pillow and looked down at the floor with surprise. No Dolly. There was no Dolly to be seen anywhere. Where had she got to? Had she flown into the hall when the doctor came in? Without anyone noticing? Or when the doctor left... Had she flown out to the hall when he left? Maybe she was now hiding between the coats on the coat rack? Or had she gone out the front door with the doctor? Mysteries... mysteries...

'I'll open the balcony door anyway,' Mrs Brightner said. 'It's too stuffy otherwise. And I'll get rid of that cat.' She grabbed the Pill

Cat by the scruff of the neck. He was still wet and sticky from all the ice cream that had fallen on his head. She carried him through Aggie's room and down the hall to the front door, where she threw him out onto the walkway.

'There,' she said. 'And if that filthy seagull dares to come back, I'll show it. You don't have any liquorice left?'

'No, Mummy.'

'Good. Eat the rest of your soup. What's that? Have you got *two* spoons? See? I did bring one after all!'

'Yes,' said Aggie. 'But it fell down... between the sheets.'

And while spooning up the cold soup she thought, *Where has Dolly got to... Where?*

There was someone else who was thinking, *Where has Dolly got to?*

It was Pluck, sitting by the window of his room in the tower, looking out and waiting. He waited and waited... but Dolly didn't come back.

Still Sick and More Chips

Pluck couldn't take it anymore. He closed the door of the tower behind him and went to the nineteenth floor, where Aggie lived. He stopped at the door to her flat, reached out to press the doorbell, then hesitated and pulled his hand back... Oh!

Of course Mrs Brightner herself would come to the door because Aggie was in bed. And Mrs Brightner would snarl at him, then slam the door in his face... He was sure of it.

Then he heard a meow behind him. The Pill Cat was sitting near the railing washing himself. He kept licking one paw and then rubbing his head with that same paw. Pluck knew the cat and said hello.

'Hello,' said the Pill Cat.

'What are you doing up here?' Pluck asked. 'Don't you live downstairs in the lobby? With the doorman?'

'It's true,' said the Pill Cat. 'But I'm up here now. It's not against the law, you know.'

'Gosh, I just asked what you were doing,' Pluck said.

'I'm licking myself clean,' the Pill Cat said. 'After such a delicious meal, I have to lick myself clean very carefully! And what a feast it was.'

'Well,' said Pluck. 'Good for you.' And he was about to walk away when a terrible thought occurred to him. The cat... right in front of Mrs Brightner's door and Dolly hadn't come back yet.

'What did you eat?' Pluck asked sharply.

'That's not really any of your business,' the Pill Cat said. 'But let me tell you, I was very lucky. I got to go in there' – he pointed at Mrs Brightner's with one paw – 'and what I got there... fantastic... I only had to reach out with one paw and *smack!*'

'Stop it! Shut up! Shut your trap, you horrible cat!' Pluck screamed angrily.

'And you were so keen to know what I ate – '

'Go away!' Pluck cried. 'And quick! Before I kick you off the walkway.'

Giving Pluck a wide berth, the Pill Cat crept off to the brick staircase.

Pluck was a bit ashamed of having snapped at him like that, but he was also very upset. Dolly had been eaten... he knew that now for sure.

Mrs Brightner had lured the Pill Cat into her flat... just when Dolly came flying in... and Aggie might have seen it all. And she was stuck in bed and couldn't do anything to help.

If only he could talk to Aggie.

He shuffled down the walkway.

Was he really sure? Had the cat really eaten lovely Dolly? Had anyone in the Pill Building seen it happen? He thought of the Stamper family who lived one floor up and ran to the big brick staircase.

A little later Pluck was catching his breath in the Stampers' living room. It was like he'd never left. The room smelt of chips again and five of the little Stampers were walking around in pyjamas.

'Are you sick again?' he asked.

'We're *still* sick,' they cried. 'We've got measles.'

'Does it last that long? When I was here... months ago –'

'My dear Pluck,' said Mr Stamper. 'You were here a week ago. Or maybe a little bit longer. Have you forgotten? Now sit down quietly on a mattress and I'll give you a plate of chips.'

Just a week ago? That was impossible. But now that Pluck thought about it, he knew it was true. It was just that such a terrible lot had happened in that week. Aggie and Dizzy and Mrs Brightner and the seagulls. And he had spent a few days at Mr Penn's, when he couldn't get into his tower.

'We watched out for you,' Mr Stamper said. 'Sometimes we saw you driving your little red truck.'

'And once we saw your pigeon,' said the smallest Stamper. 'We saw Dolly. Here, right in front of our window. She flew past with a little basket in her beak. What was in the basket?'

Pluck gave a deep sigh.

'Nothing nasty's happened, has it? What's wrong?'

He told the Stampers about Aggie being sick and what had happened with the airlift. They were all stunned. They stopped eating and were deathly silent for half a minute and then they all started shouting at the same time.

'I don't believe it!' 'That pigeon's way too fast. A cat could never catch her!'

'No, never!' 'Yes, it could!' 'No, it couldn't.' 'No, not usually, but if she had a basket.' 'Not even with a basket!'

'Quiet!' Mr Stamper shouted. 'Don't all blabber at once! One thing's certain, Pluck, you don't know for sure. That Pill Cat's always boasting. You can't trust him. Who knows, maybe Dolly will arrive any moment now. Maybe she's already waiting for you on the rail next to your tower.'

Pluck shook his head. 'I don't think so,' he said. 'It's not like Dolly to stay away this long. She always came straight back to tell me how it went and usually she had a letter from Aggie too. If only I could talk to Aggie, but I'm too scared to ring her doorbell. Maybe one of you?' He looked around hesitantly.

'One of us?' Mr Stamper cried. 'Ring Mrs Brightner's doorbell?'

'Are you too scared too?'

'Um... not exactly scared... but she won't let us in. She'll slam the door in our faces. She's done it before. I think she thinks we're dirty.'

'Then I'll have to wait till Aggie's better and allowed out again,' Pluck said. 'And all that time I won't know what's happened to Dolly.'

'Come on, your chips are getting cold,' Mr Stamper said.

Pluck took a forkful of chips to please Mr Stamper. They tasted good but he found it very hard to swallow.

TV

Why don't you eat a little more?' Mr Stamper asked Pluck.

'I'm not really hungry,' Pluck said. 'I have to get home.'

'You leaving already?' the little Stampers moaned. 'Aren't you going to stay and watch TV with us?'

'Let him be,' Mr Stamper said. 'He's sad, can't you see that? That criminal cat ate his pigeon. And now he doesn't feel like chips and he doesn't feel like watching TV either. Besides you have to go back to bed, the lot of you. You're sick.'

'Not me!' the smallest Stamper shouted. 'I'm not sick.'

'You have to go to bed too,' Mr Stamper said. 'Isn't it strange that the doctor hasn't come today? He promised he would. Anyway, into bed, all of you. And you can watch TV in bed. I've already turned it on. Are you sure you won't stay for a while, Pluck?'

'No, really,' Pluck said. 'Thanks for everything and I'll see you later!'

But after Pluck was out on the walkway, the smallest Stamper came running after him, panting, 'Could you come back for a minute, please? Our TV's not working.'

'Why do I have to come back because of that?' Pluck asked.

'We thought... you're so smart...' the little Stamper said, 'maybe you can fix it for us.'

'Me? I don't know the first thing about TV sets,' Pluck said. 'Nothing at all!'

'Please,' said the little Stamper. 'Just have a look.'

Sighing, Pluck went back into the flat.

The little Stampers and their dad were crowded around the TV set.

'Pluck's back! Pluck will get it going again!' they cried.

'I really don't know anything about TVs,' Pluck said. 'You'll have to get a repairman.

It's much too complicated for ordinary people because –' Then he noticed the cord dangling down. The TV wasn't plugged in. He plugged it in. A second later the sound came on. And then the picture.

'See!' the Stampers all screamed. 'Pluck fixed it!'

And Mr Stamper shook his hand and said, 'Thanks a lot, son.'

'It's nothing,' Pluck said. And he was about to say goodbye for the second time, when he heard one of the Stampers shout, 'The doctor! There's the doctor!'

Pluck looked around and couldn't see any doctors anywhere, but the little Stamper pointed at the TV screen.

'Well, I'll be!' Mr Stamper cried. 'It's our doctor. No wonder he couldn't come today. He had to appear on TV. What's he going to do? Shhhh... boys, be quiet!'

Pluck stopped a moment to listen. He knew the doctor, who always came to see people in the Pill Building when they were

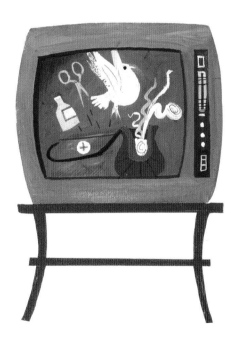

sick. Apparently he was going to give a talk about measles.

'Hello, mums and dads,' the doctor said. 'As you know, measles is a childhood disease. It's not serious, so there's no need to worry. Children always get better. And now I'll show you the tablets I give to children with measles.' The doctor put his bag on the small table in front of him. He opened the bag and pulled out a large packet of bandages and right after that a big fat pigeon flew out of the bag.

The little Stampers all cheered and cried out, 'He's doing magic tricks! The doctor's a magician!'

But Pluck was frozen to the spot for a mo-ment and then screamed louder than anyone, 'Dolly! It's Dolly!'

He fell full-length on the mattress floor and kicked his legs and laughed and screamed and cried all at once.

'Shhh... be quiet!' Mr Stamper said. 'Let's see what's happening.'

The doctor too was extremely surprised. For a while he looked around in horror without saying a word. The pigeon had dis-appeared off screen and the doctor started again.

'Please excuse me, mums and dads,' he said. 'Without my knowing it, this pigeon concealed itself in my bag. The bird has been immediately released outside and I can now continue my talk about measles.'

'I'm going,' Pluck said.

'Wait a minute,' Mr Stamper said. 'There's no rush! She still has to fly all the way from the TV studio! That's miles and miles.'

'I know,' Pluck said. 'But I want to be there when she gets back home.'

He waved a quick goodbye and ran out the door on his way to the tower.

Going up the stairs he saw the Pill Cat. The

cat shrank anxiously when it saw Pluck.

'Don't be scared,' Pluck said. 'I won't hurt you. But you did tell me a very mean lie.'

'Did I lie to you?' the cat asked. 'What did I say?'

'You said that you...' Pluck fell silent. The cat had never said he'd eaten Dolly. Pluck had just suspected it.

'Forget it...' Pluck said.

He stopped for a moment at the door to his tower, leant out over the railing and peered into the sky.

The evening came and it started to get dark. Pluck waited and waited.

And only when it had grown so dark that he couldn't see into the distance anymore, did he hear the flapping of wings just before Dolly landed next to him, exhausted and slightly tattered.

'Water...' she said weakly.

Pluck fetched a saucer of water for her and a bit of sweet corn and that perked her up.

'I was shut in a bag for ever so long,' she said. 'I almost suffocated.'

'How'd you get in the bag?' Pluck asked. 'Tell me!'

'At Aggie's... The doctor was at Aggie's and I was under the bed. And I had to hide somewhere... and then the bag was open, so I snuck into it. And I thought... *He'll go see another patient and then he'll open the bag again.* But he didn't, he drove a really long way in his car and it took a really long time... and then the bag opened and I was in a big room with enormous bright lights... and there were men... I don't know what it was.'

'It was the TV studio,' Pluck said. 'And you were on TV. I saw you.'

'Me? On TV? Did you see me?'

'I saw you fly out of the bag.'

Dolly forgot how tired she was and what a terrible day it had been. She swelled with pride.

'I'm a TV pigeon,' she said. 'Am I famous now, Pluck?'

'I think so,' Pluck said. 'At least for today. But best of all, you're back home safe and sound.'

The Monkey Chain

'I'd really love to know how Aggie's going,' Pluck said. 'And I think Aggie would like to hear from us too.'

'I'll fly down to her balcony,' Dolly said bravely. 'I'm not scared.'

'No,' Pluck cried. 'Please, don't! I think I'll go visit the Stamper family.'

The little Stampers were very happy to see Pluck.

Mr Stamper had his apron on again and he was back in the kitchen. This time he wasn't making chips. He was making bean soup.

'Sit down, Pluck! Yes, that's right, on the floor! Ignore the mess. A man alone with so many kids... Mess happens. Would you like a bowl of bean soup?'

'Yes, please,' Pluck said. 'Are you all better now? Have you got over your measles?'

'We're better and we're going to the beach. The doctor said we all have to go to the seaside for a while.'

'That'll be fun,' Pluck said. And in between eating his soup with meatballs, he told them about Aggie. Aggie who was still sick and lived one floor down. Just below them.

'Isn't there some way to get down to her balcony?' he asked. 'Couldn't I climb down from your balcony to hers?'

'No, no, impossible!' Mr Stamper cried. 'It's much too high up. And there's nothing to hold on to... All that slippery concrete... Look for yourself!' He took Pluck out onto the balcony. 'See,' he said. 'You can only see a tiny corner of Aggie's balcony. See how high up we are?'

Pluck looked down and felt a little scared. They were on the twentieth floor. He could see that climbing down was completely out of the question.

Then the smallest Stamper came up to them and said, 'Dad, why don't we do the monkey chain?'

'What? Oh, no... we can't do that. Pluck wouldn't dare do that.'

But all of his brothers came up and started jumping around shouting, 'Yes, he would. He's not scared! The monkey chain, the monkey chain!'

'What's the monkey chain?' Pluck asked.

'No, no...' Mr Stamper said. 'It just happened that once we dropped a ball off our balcony. And it landed on the balcony below ours. We didn't dare to ring Mrs Brightner's doorbell, you know... because we're a bit scared of her.'

'Yes,' said Pluck. 'I know the feeling.'

'Well, then we made a monkey chain... How exactly did it go, boys?'

'We'll show you, Pluck. Come here, we'll make one for you!'

In the flat below, Aggie was still stuck in bed. She was allowed to get up for a couple of hours each day, but she wasn't allowed outside.

And now she was lying in front of the open balcony door and looking out at the blue sky.

If she saw a bird fly past, she sat up, hoping it might be Dolly the pigeon. But it was never Dolly.

She was desperate to find out what had happened to Dolly. Where had she got to? Was Dolly still alive? And how were things with Pluck? Did he think about her sometimes? Or was he too busy...

Aggie lay there in bed worrying and fretting and feeling very miserable. *I'll just go back to sleep...* she thought, closing her eyes.

'Pssst! Aggie!' a voice whispered close by. Aggie jumped and sat up straight.

A head was dangling down in front of her balcony door. An upside-down head! It was bright red.

'Pluck!' Aggie exclaimed.

'Hello,' said the head, with difficulty. 'How are you?'

'ok,' said Aggie. 'Quick, tell me if Dolly's safe.'

'Dolly's fine,' Pluck said. 'She's back. She snuck into the doctor's bag.'

'Oh, that's where she got to!' said Aggie. 'What's holding you up?'

'I'm on the end of a monkey chain,' Pluck said. 'There are three Stampers above me. But I can't keep it up for much longer! Are you almost better?'

'Yes,' said Aggie. 'The doctor says I have to go to the seaside. But my mother won't take me. She's scared of seagulls.'

'I can understand that... Hey, I can feel them pulling me up... Bye.'

'Quick,' said Aggie, 'My mother's coming...'

Pluck's head disappeared just in time.

'Who were you talking to?' Mrs Brightner asked as she came into the room.

'I was just singing to myself...' Aggie said. 'Because I'm so glad to be better.'

Pluck was back on his feet on the Stampers' balcony.

'Now you know what the monkey chain is,' said the little Stampers. 'Wasn't it fantastic? Did you get to talk to her?'

'Yes,' Pluck said, still bright red from the exertion. 'She's almost better. And the doctor said she should go to the seaside for a while.'

'Just like us,' said the smallest Stamper.

'The doctor said we have to go to the seaside too.'

'Would it be all right if Aggie went with you?' Pluck asked.

'Of course,' said Mr Stamper. 'It would be fine by us, but will her mother let her?'

'Um, will you ask Mrs Brightner?' Pluck asked.

'What? Me? You want me to ask Mrs

Brightner something?' Mr Stamper exclaimed in horror. 'Oh no, I wouldn't dare. No, no, no. You ask her.'

'Me?' Pluck said. 'I'll never dare to ask her mother anything again.'

'Let's think for a moment...' Mr Stamper said. 'Is there anyone in the Pill Building who'd dare to ask her?'

'Maybe the doctor,' said the smallest Stamper.

'Of course! The doctor! You go to the doctor's surgery, Pluck. And discuss it with him. But eat another bowl of soup first.'

'I'd love to,' Pluck said. Because the monkey chain had made him hungry.

'And...' Mr Stamper said, 'if we go to the seaside, all of us, including Aggie... would you like to come with us? We've got a beach house on the edge of the dunes. And we're going to drive there.'

'Then I'll come to stay with you for a few days,' Pluck said. 'And I'll drive there in my own tow truck.'

One Tidy Afternoon

The doctor lived on the first floor of the Pill Building. There was a long line of chairs in front of his door with all the people who had come to see him sitting on them. They went in one at a time. And the last one to go in was a boy.

'So,' said the doctor. 'Tell me, what's wrong with you?'

'Nothing,' said the boy.

'Nothing? What are you doing here then?'

'There's something I'd like to ask...'

'What would you like to ask? Make it quick though, because I'm busy... Wait a minute, aren't you Pluck?'

'Yes,' said Pluck.

'I know you,' the doctor said. 'I've seen you driving around in your tow truck. Tell me, what's it about?'

'It's about Aggie Brightner,' Pluck said.

'Aggie? She's one of my patients. She's just had measles and I think she should go to the seaside for a while, but her mother won't even consider it.'

'That's just it, doctor,' Pluck said. 'The Stampers are going to the seaside. They'd be happy to take Aggie with them.'

'The Stampers? Quite right. They had measles too. Excellent, that's just perfect. Aggie can go with the Stamper family.'

'We'd all love it if she could,' Pluck said. 'But nobody's brave enough to ask.'

'Brave enough to ask what? And who do you have to ask?'

'Brave enough to ask Mrs Brightner if

Aggie can come with us,' Pluck said.

'Really?' said the doctor. 'How silly! Although... I can imagine it. Mrs Brightner can be rather difficult. But you know what... I'll go up there right away. I'll ask her. And I'll let you know.'

When the doctor arrived at Mrs Brightner's, she was in the middle of scrubbing the floor. She was kneeling down next to a bucket of soapsuds and she'd put Aggie on top of a cabinet until she was finished.

'Could you stand on that rag please, doctor?' Mrs Brightner asked. 'I'm just giving the lino a scrub, you see.'

'I do see,' the doctor said. 'And I understand. It was high time.'

Mrs Brightner was shocked and put the scrubbing brush down for a moment. 'Do you really think so?' she asked. 'Did you think it was dirty in here?'

'Oh...' the doctor hesitated. 'I wouldn't say dirty... but...' He ran a finger over a chair and screwed up his nose. 'It would be a very good thing if you could give the whole flat a thorough clean.'

'But I've done that, doctor!' Mrs Brightner cried. 'In the springtime! I gave the whole place a big spring cleaning!'

'And it's so grimy already,' the doctor sighed. 'What a shame!'

'You must realise...' Mrs Brightner said, 'with a child in the house things always get dirty much sooner.'

'That's true,' the doctor said. 'Wouldn't it

be wonderful if Aggie went away for a few weeks. Then you'd have all the time in the world to clean the house. And the sea air would do Aggie the world of good.'

'But I couldn't possibly send her off to the seaside by herself.'

'No, of course not. But, by coincidence, I happen to know a family that would like to take her to the seaside with them. A highly respectable family.'

'Really?'

'Yes, just imagine! You could spend four whole weeks cleaning. Mopping out the whole house. Emptying out all of the cupboards. Washing the curtains.'

Mrs Brightner's mouth started to water. 'It would be a dream come true,' she said. 'Who are these people who would like to take Aggie with them?'

'The Stamper family from upstairs.'

'The Stampers!' Mrs Brightner cried indignantly. 'Oh, no. Never.'

'Why not? Do you know them?'

'I don't *know* them, but I've heard they're very messy. They keep an untidy home and they all have long messy hair. That's what people say.'

'Well,' said the doctor. 'I've been there quite a few times recently because all of the boys have had measles. All except one. But I've never noticed anything messy about them. I didn't notice a thing.'

'No?' Mrs Brightner said. 'Maybe it's a good idea after all. You know what, doctor? I'll go there myself. I'll go up there personally to see if they keep a clean and tidy house.'

'That sounds like an excellent idea,' the doctor said. 'I'll tell them you'll be dropping by later for afternoon tea. Goodbye, Mrs Brightner. Bye, Aggie!'

When the doctor came out the front door, Pluck was on the walkway.

'Did she say yes?' Pluck asked.

'She's coming to visit this afternoon,' the doctor said. 'Go straight to Mr Stamper and help him tidy up. Mrs Brightner wants to make sure they're a respectable family. You have to make sure it works out. Good luck!'

Pluck ran upstairs and found the Stamper family in even more chaos than usual. The kids were in the middle of a ferocious pillow fight and downy feathers were floating through the room. The mattresses on the floor were littered with bread crusts from breakfast and someone had knocked over a large teapot.

When Mr Stamper heard that Aggie's mother was coming to visit, he lifted his arms in despair.

'Impossible!' he cried. 'How could anyone get this place neat and tidy in a couple of hours?'

'I know what to do,' Pluck said. 'We'll leave this room shut. We'll just tidy up the hall and that side room. I'll help.'

'Boys!' Mr Stamper yelled, 'Get the hose!'

They slaved away, spraying with the hose until the small side room and the hall were clean. Then they scrubbed and rubbed and polished until everything was shining.

They threw all the junk in the big room, which they left just as it was.

And when Mrs Brightner arrived in the afternoon, they showed her into a small room that was squeaky clean.

Mr Stamper was sitting there with all the little Stampers, who were lined up as if a photographer was about to arrive. They had brushed their hair and combed it neatly, and they were all wearing shirts and ties, and after Mrs Brightner had sat down they all drank tea with their little fingers poking out.

'Isn't it nice and tidy here?' Aggie's mother said. 'I hear you have a beach house in Egham-on-Sea.'

'Yes, Mrs Brightner,' said Mr Stamper. 'A very tidy little beach house.'

'And you're going there by car?'

'Yes, Mrs Brightner, a tidy car.'

'And you'll make sure Aggie doesn't get dirty on the beach?'

'Dirty?' cried Mr Stamper in horror. 'Does that girl get dirty? Oh, she can't come with us then. Girls who get dirty... no... I'm afraid we'll have to call the whole thing off.'

'Oh, no, not at all,' Mrs Brightner exclaimed, blushing. 'I'll tell her she must stay spotless the whole time.'

'All right then,' Mr Stamper said. 'We're going Tuesday morning. Send her here first thing. With her suitcase.'

'That's arranged then,' said Mrs Brightner. 'I'll be on my way. Thank you very much for the tea. And I think you keep a very respectable home.'

Mrs Brightner left. And it was a good thing she hadn't seen the big living room...

Off to Egham-on-Sea

Pluck woke up with a start and looked at his alarm clock. It was already seven o'clock! He'd overslept. The Stampers were going to leave in their car at six with Aggie. And he'd promised to go with them. Of course, he was going to drive in his own little tow truck, but he was supposed to follow them. And now he was an hour too late.

Pluck got dressed in three seconds flat. He picked up the empty drawing-pin box and said to Zaza, 'Quick, get into your box. We're going!'

'Do you mind if I stay home?' Zaza asked. 'Sea air is very bad for cockroaches.'

'But you'll be alone for ages,' Pluck said. 'Maybe a whole week.'

'That doesn't matter,' Zaza said. 'Just leave me a few pieces of apple peel. And make sure you lock the door properly so no one can get in. Bye.'

'You sure?' Pluck asked.

'Absolutely,' Zaza whispered sleepily. 'I'd rather be alone than at the seaside.'

Pluck said goodbye and left with his small suitcase. He locked the tower from the outside with three keys and ran to the lift. But outside on the street there was no sign of the Stampers. They'd already left.

I'll drive really fast, thought Pluck. *Maybe I can catch up before they get there.*

He climbed into his tow truck. It was still nice and quiet on the streets this early in the morning and he sped off and turned right at the first corner and – there was the Stampers'

car. Pluck stopped immediately.

It was a horribly ancient car full of little Stampers.

The six boys were sitting in the car with Aggie. The suitcases and bags and lots of other things they hadn't been able to fit inside were on the roof. At the front, Mr Stamper was hard at work with the crank. The car was so old-fashioned you had to start it with a crank.

'We've broken down,' Mr Stamper moaned. 'We've broken down already! Half a block from home and the car won't move an inch. It won't go. The engine stalled and no matter what I do, I can't get it started again. Would you believe it? It's worked perfectly for fifty-eight years. It used to be my grandfather's. And now it's broken down all of a sudden. It's unbelievable.'

'Never mind,' Pluck said. 'I've got a tow truck. I can tow you.'

But after they'd hooked up a cable and Pluck had got into his tow truck and tried to drive off... nothing happened. Nothing budged. His tow truck was only little. It was too small to pull the Stamper's big, heavy car.

'Can't we all go in your truck?' the little Stampers asked.

'Of course not,' Pluck said. 'And definitely not with all those bags.'

'What if we push?' said Aggie. 'I don't mind pushing.'

'Push? All the way to Egham? That'll take us weeks,' Mr Stamper growled. 'No, we'll

have to think of something else. Come on, let's sit down on the pavement and think about it.'

They sat there on the pavement with their heads hanging. Six little Stampers with their dad and Aggie and Pluck, all in a row. They thought and thought and they all jumped when a gruff voice shouted, 'What's all this about?'

It was the Major. He was sitting on a very long horse with his adjutant. The horse was called Longmount, Pluck knew him well.

'What's going on?' the Major asked. 'Has that old rattletrap died on you?'

'It's not a rattletrap,' Mr Stamper said. 'It's a fabulous car that's been running for almost sixty years. But now it's broken down and we have to go to Egham!'

'I see,' said the Major. 'Well, I could give you a ride on my horse. The little ones can all get on my horse. I'll take you to Egham!'

But now Longmount started to splutter. 'No! That's way too many. I'll sag!'

'Balderdash, horse,' said the Major. 'We've got "the wheels", haven't we? Adjutant, fetch the wheels this instant.'

Pluck was very curious what kind of wheels they were and where they would put them, but when the adjutant came back he worked it out immediately. It was a very practical undercarriage with wheels at the bottom and straps to go around Longmount's middle.

'There,' said the Major. 'Now let's get you all sorted. The bags go in the truck along with Mr Stamper. And the rest on my horse.'

'Ow, ow, I'm starting to sag,' Longmount cried as Aggie and the six little Stampers climbed up onto his back, but the Major said, 'Stop moaning! Your tummy is resting on wheels, what more do you want? If you get tired, lift up your legs, then you can roll along without any effort at all. And you should be glad to do something for Pluck for once! He rescued you when you were stuck in the canal!'

'That's true,' said Longmount, who was a little ashamed of himself and started walking like a good horse.

It was a very strange sight.

Pluck drove at the front with Mr Stamper in his tow truck, which was crammed with bags and packages.

Behind them came Longmount with the Major and the six little Stampers plus Aggie. The poor adjutant got left behind and stood there on the pavement saluting.

Fortunately the weather was beautiful. But it took them most of the day to get to Egham because besides being a very slow horse, Longmount was also a terrible moaner who wanted to rest every hour. When they finally saw the sea, the Stampers all cheered like crazy and Aggie wanted to jump into the water straightaway, but Mr Stamper said, 'First the

beach house!' He pointed to a small wooden house at the bottom of the dunes, close to the beach and close to the lighthouse.

'Will you stay here with us tonight, Major? You can if you'd like. It sleeps ten.'

'Very kind of you,' the Major said, 'but I'm going back to the Pill Building. Ready, horse. About turn!'

They thanked the Major and waved good-bye. Then they went into the house.

It was the nicest little house Pluck had ever seen. It had just two rooms, one living room and a small kitchen, and there were ten hammocks hung up in the living room.

'One each,' Mr Stamper said. 'And one spare hammock in case someone comes to stay. You never know.'

By the time they'd unpacked their bags, it was eight o'clock in the evening and the sun was starting to go down.

'We've got time for a quick dip,' said Mr Stamper. 'We'll just jump in and out again.'

And that's what they did. Six Stampers and Aggie and Pluck, hand in hand in the big waves. It was freezing cold and fabulous and they all looked pink in the light of the setting sun.

When they'd come out again and dried themselves off, Pluck saw something on the beach. It was pink too. A big, beautiful shell. He put it in his pocket. Half an hour later they were all sound asleep in the hammocks and dreaming of tall, wild waves.

The Tootenlisp

They'd been at the Stampers' beach house for three days now. Three fantastic, warm, sunny days and they had spent all their time in the water or playing on the beach.

The house itself was tiny, with just a living room and a little kitchen, but it was cosy and they all slept in hammocks. Each of the six little Stampers had his own hammock. There was one for Mr Stamper too and one for Pluck and one for Aggie. And there was also an empty hammock. That was a spare. In case someone came to stay.

On the morning of the fourth day, Mr Stamper woke everyone up.

'There's a gale blowing!' he shouted. 'Look!'

They all got out of their hammocks and looked out of the window.

The wind was raging around the house, there was no sun and sand was blowing up against the windows. You could hear the waves booming. It was a bit scary.

'And we don't have a thing to eat!' Mr Stamper cried. 'We haven't got anything for

breakfast. We can't go to the village to do the shopping in this weather.'

'I'll go,' Pluck said. 'In my tow truck.'

'In a storm like this?' Mr Stamper said. 'Are you sure?'

'It'll be fun,' Pluck said. He got into his truck with a shopping list and a big bag and drove to the village.

The wind was terribly strong. Pluck had to hold on to his cap and sand blew in his eyes and he could hardly see a thing. But Pluck didn't give up easily and he kept going.

He bought all the things on his list in the village supermarket. Bread and margarine and cheese and jam and lots of other things. His bag was bulging and on top there were nine ice lollies. One each.

Then he drove back.

I have to go a bit faster, Pluck thought, *otherwise the lollies will melt. You know what, I'll take this narrow little track straight through the dunes. That will be much shorter.* And he turned onto the path through the dunes.

The tow truck drove bravely through the sand. But the storm was so wild and the sand swirled so much that after five minutes Pluck couldn't even make out the path and *brrrm*! His truck stopped with a jerk.

He was stuck in a pile of sand.

Pluck climbed out and tried to push and tug, but he couldn't move the truck at all.

I'll have to walk back. It can't be helped...

He picked up the heavy bag and started trudging through the dunes. And then his cap blew off. Pluck ran after it, but when he almost had it, the wind blew sand in his eyes. He had to put down the bag and when he could see again his cap was gone. Even worse, he didn't know which way to go anymore. He didn't even know which direction the sea was. There were tall sand dunes all around him.

Thick dark clouds raced across the sky, he couldn't see the sun and he was lost.

With the heavy bag hanging from one arm, Pluck trudged up a dune and down the other side. But behind it he only found more dunes

and he got so tired from pushing through the sand and fighting the wind that he sat down in a sheltered hollow and said, 'Now I don't have a clue. I'm lost and they'll never find me. I'll have to wait here until the storm dies down and that could take a whole week. There's no one around to ask directions. Not even a seagull.'

It was a scary feeling to be all alone in the storm with all that sand. But he had the bag of shopping next to him and that was comforting.

At least I won't die of hunger, thought Pluck. *I've got enough food here for a whole month.* He listened carefully to see if he could hear the sound of the sea through the roaring of the wind...

If only he knew which way the sea was.

And then... between two gusts of wind... he heard a sound. Close by: *Toooootooooo.* And then another *toooo-toooo.* It sounded like the time signal on the radio.

It's like I've got a radio in my pocket, thought Pluck. *But I don't have a radio with me.*

He felt his pocket. The shell! The big, beautiful, pink shell he found on the beach the very first day!

He held the shell up to his ear. Yes! It was definitely the shell. *Toooo-toooo.* He kept listening.

Then the tooting stopped and a very soft, whispery voice came out of the shell.

The voice said, 'The thee'th there.'

Pluck looked around, half expecting to see a thief sneaking up to steal his shopping. But the voice continued, 'Right ahead, between thothe treeth.'

Now Pluck realised what the shell was talking about. It meant, 'The sea's there. Right ahead between those trees.'

It lisped a little and said TH when it meant S. Pluck picked up the shopping bag and walked between the two trees, still holding the shell up to one ear.

'Keep going for the thee,' said the shell.

'Thank you,' Pluck said.

He stared deep into the shell for a moment to see if there was an animal inside it. But no,

it was an empty shell. There wasn't anything inside it at all.

'Keep going. Thoon you'll thee the thee.'

'I'll soon see the sea,' said Pluck. 'Thank you.' And he kept going straight ahead over the top of the highest dune and then he saw the sea. He also saw the beach and the lighthouse and the long breakwater where they'd gone for a swim. Now he could find his way back to the Stampers' beach house and he was very relieved and said, 'Thanks a lot! Can you always find the way? Do you ever get lost?'

'I never get lotht,' the shell said. 'I'm the Tootenlithp.'

'The Tootenlisp? What a great name! From now on, I'll keep you with me all the time. Then I'll never get lost again either. Tell me... how come you always know the way?'

But the Tootenlisp just said 'toot' twice and then fell silent.

Pluck trudged through the wet sand on the beach to get back to the house.

The entire Stamper family was standing at the window with Aggie looking out for him. With loud cries they pulled him into the house.

'Pluck without a cap!' they yelled.

'Pluck without a tow truck! What happened?'

'At least he's got the shopping,' Mr Stamper said. 'Tell us what happened!'

Pluck told them about his truck getting stuck. And getting lost. But he didn't tell them about the Tootenlisp. That was *his* secret.

Now he had a shell that could always tell him which way to go, no matter where he was. And that was a very good feeling.

'As soon as the storm dies down, we'll go and pull your truck out of the sand,' Mr Stamper said. 'And find your cap. But first we're going to have breakfast, because we're starving. Hey! What are those nine sticks doing on top of the shopping?'

'They're... they're the ice lollies,' Pluck said. 'Oh, what a pain! They've melted.'

Shirley in the Oil Slick

It was a beautiful, warm, sunny morning in Egham-on-Sea. The little Stampers were playing on the beach. Pluck and Aggie had been for a swim and were sitting in the tow truck ready to drive to the village to get some bread from the baker's.

Just when they were about to drive off, they heard a frightened screech.

Pluck looked around, but couldn't see anyone.

'Up in the sky,' said Aggie.

Pluck looked up. And hovering overhead was a big white seagull. Carl! It was Carl with the wooden leg.

'Ahoy!' he called.

'Ahoy!' Pluck shouted back.

'Come quickly!' Carl screeched. 'Help, help!'

'What's wrong? What's the matter? Come down here. I can't understand what you're saying.'

Carl landed on the tow truck and said, 'Shirley's in the oil.'

'Who's Shirley?' Pluck asked.

'My sister. She's in the oil.'

'Where? What kind of oil?'

'In the sea,' Carl said. 'There... along the beach, near that breakwater. You know the one I mean? That's where she is, my poor sister. She went for a paddle and got caught in an oil slick. She can't get back out. She's trapped in a big clump of seaweed and muck and dirty black oil. Come on, hurry. Maybe you can rescue her with your tow truck!'

'You fly ahead,' Pluck said. 'Lead the way.'

He turned the truck around and drove over the beach with Aggie. Carl flew in front of them and led them to the big stone breakwater that ran out into the sea.

'She's right at the end of the breakwater,' Carl cried. 'You have to drive out to the end.'

'I'm coming,' Pluck said. But driving over those gigantic boulders wasn't easy. They had to keep stopping to push and tug at the truck, while Carl flew overhead nervously, screeching, 'Hurry, hurry!'

Finally they made it to the end of the breakwater. They looked down and there she was! Poor Shirley, sitting in the oil that was floating on the water. She was stuck, that was obvious. She couldn't move an inch. And her screeching was lot more impatient than her brother's.

'You gonna help me or not?' she cried.

'We're doing our best,' Pluck shouted back.

Slowly he lowered the big claw until it was dangling in the oil slick. Then he closed it carefully and lifted Shirley up together with an enormous clump of seaweed and rubbish and greasy black oil. The whole lot came down *splat* on the back of his truck. Oil and mud splashed all over Pluck and Aggie, but that didn't matter, because they didn't have their clothes on anyway. 'Take me to my nest!' Shirley shrieked. 'Now!'

'OK,' Pluck said. 'Where's your nest?'

'There. In the dunes. Just over that ridge,

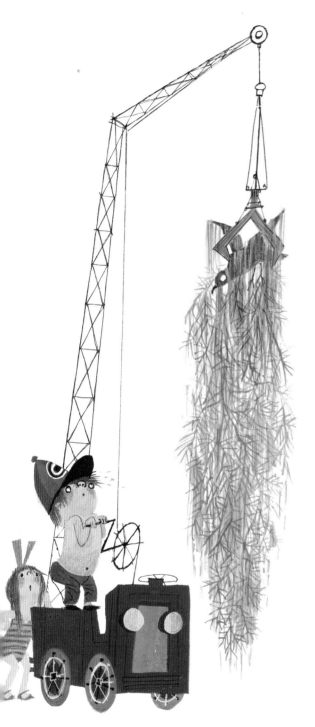

that's where my nest is. With five eggs.'

'Calm down, Shirl,' her brother Carl said. 'You can't go back to your nest like that. You need to get clean first. We'll take you to the house.'

'No!' Shirley shrieked. 'I have to get back to my eggs. Now!'

'You can't,' Carl said. 'Go on, Pluck, drive back to the house.'

'What am I supposed to do?' Pluck said. 'If you keep arguing, I don't know what to do.'

But now, for the first time, Aggie spoke up. 'I think Carl's right,' she said. 'Shirley can't go and sit on her eggs like that. Mr Stamper has to clean her up first.'

Pluck drove straight to the house while Shirley ranted and raved. 'If my eggs go cold, it's your fault,' she said. 'Nitwits.'

'Just lay some new eggs,' Carl said.

'What? Did you hear that? Is that any way to talk to a mother?' Shirley shrieked.

'You're not a mother yet,' Carl said. 'When the little seagulls hatch out, then you'll be a mother. But they're aren't any yet, so you're not a mother.'

Carl and his sister got into a terrible fight about whether or not Shirley was a mother, but then they arrived at the beach house and the whole Stamper family came outside.

'What's that?' the little Stampers shouted. 'Yuck. What a mess...'

But Mr Stamper understood immediately and said, 'I see what's happened. Another poor bird got caught in the oil. Bring it here and I'll clean the poor thing off.'

'What about my nest?' Shirley sobbed. 'My eggs will go cold.'

'We'll fetch your eggs here,' Mr Stamper said. 'Then you can hatch them out on the porch. Come here,' he said to the youngest Stamper. 'Run like lightning to the dunes and get this seagull's nest. Eggs and all.'

'I'll show him where it is,' Carl said. He flew off and the little Stamper ran along behind him as fast as his legs could carry him.

Now that she knew her eggs were coming, Shirley calmed down a little and let them clean her. They put her in a tub and scrubbed her off feather by feather. It took a really long time and Shirley was not an easy-going seagull. She struggled a few times and even pecked Mr Stamper on the nose.

'Where are my eggs?' she cried. 'It's taking too long. I'm clean now. I want to go to them.'

'That's out of the question,' Mr Stamper said firmly. 'You're clean now, but you have to stay here a few days to recover.'

'I'm not sick,' said Shirley.

'Your feathers are sick. A bird that gets stuck in oil has sick feathers.' But Shirley whined so much that Pluck and Aggie went outside to see if the smallest Stamper was on his way with the eggs.

Finally… at last… yes, there he was, walking up and all out of breath.

Carl was flying above him.

'Got them?' Pluck asked. 'You haven't got them! Where are they?'

'Th-th-they were gone,' the little Stamper puffed. 'The nest was empty.'

'Stolen!' screeched Carl. 'The boys stole them!'

'What boys?' Pluck asked.

'I saw them running off,' Carl said. 'The boys who always steal eggs.'

'Why?' Aggie asked. 'What do they do with them?'

'They sell them to the baker.'

'To the baker? Here in Egham? What's the baker do with them?'

'He makes egg custard,' Carl groaned. 'Now we have to go and tell Shirley that her babies are in the custard tarts.'

'No, don't!' Aggie said. 'Don't tell her that.

Come on, Pluck, we were going to the baker's anyway. 'Let's go and get Shirley's eggs back.'

'OK, we need to hurry,' Pluck said, climbing into the truck with Aggie.

Carl with the wooden leg went into the house.

'Where are they?' Shirley cried. 'Where are my eggs?'

'They're on the way,' Carl said. 'They're coming. They're bringing them.'

'Look me in the eye,' Shirley said. 'Is that true?' But Carl didn't dare to look Shirley in the eye. 'It's true…' he said feebly. 'Honest…'

The whole family had to hold Shirley back, otherwise she would have attacked her brother.

Shirley's Eggs

Shirley the seagull was at her wits' end because her eggs had disappeared. She got so furious and so ferocious that Mr Stamper had to lock her up in the wardrobe.

And where had the eggs got to? They had been stolen by boys. Who might have sold them to the baker so that he could use them to make egg custard...

Pluck drove to the village in his tow truck with Aggie. He was going much too fast, he was speeding, but he was in a big hurry. He wanted to get to the baker's as fast as he could... It might not be too late. Fortunately the road to the village was very quiet and they were there in five minutes.

They went into the baker's, where the baker's wife was standing behind the counter.

'One loaf of white bread and two loaves of brown, please,' said Pluck.

'Here you are,' she said. 'Anything else?'

'No, thank you,' Pluck said. 'Or, um... yes, there is something. Do you happen to have seagull eggs?'

'Seagull eggs? Of course not. Shops don't have seagull eggs. You have to go to the dunes for seagull eggs.'

'Yes,' said Pluck. 'But I thought you might just happen to have some. And if you did, I'd like to buy them off you.'

'Why would I have seagull eggs?' the baker's wife asked. 'You don't think we use seagull eggs, do you? To make egg custard or something like that? Is that what you think?'

Pluck felt like saying, Yes, that's exactly what I think! But the baker's wife glared at him and he was too scared to say another word.

'Anything else?' she asked.

'Yes,' Aggie said. 'Ten fresh bread rolls, please.'

The baker's wife went through a door that led to the bakery. When she opened the door they felt a gust of hot air from the enormous oven.

They saw the baker at work with big bowls of dough. A delicious smell of warm, fresh bread wafted out towards them and then the baker's wife came back with ten bread rolls, closing the door behind her.

They paid and left the shop.

'I saw them!' Aggie cried when they were back out on the street.

'What? Shirley's eggs?'

'I saw a bowl with eggs in it,' Aggie said. 'Right next to the oven. Didn't you see it?'

'No,' Pluck said. 'Were they seagull eggs?'

'They must have been,' Aggie said. 'They were way too small for chicken eggs. Oh, Pluck... what can we do? How do we get them back? Can't you sneak in and grab them? There's a back door that leads right into the bakery. Are you brave enough?'

'But the baker's standing there at the oven,' Pluck said. 'I can't go in and swipe a bowl of eggs from right under his nose.'

And then they heard lots of excited voices in the high street, calling out, 'Pluck! Aggie! Hello!'

It was the Stampers. They had walked to the village in case Pluck and Aggie needed some help.'

'Did you get Shirley's eggs?' Mr Stamper asked.

'No,' Pluck said gloomily.

'But they're in there!' Aggie shouted. 'I saw them with my own two eyes. In the bakery!'

'Are you sure?' Mr Stamper asked.

'No,' said Aggie. 'Not entirely. But I'm almost sure.'

'Then we'll have to come up with something,' Mr Stamper said. 'Let's sit down on the pavement and think.'

They sat down for quite a while, but could not think of anything.

'Look,' Pluck said. 'There's Carl on the roof of the bandstand.'

'Yes,' Mr Stamper said. 'He flew here with us.'

'I know!' cried the oldest little Stamper. 'We'll give a concert on the bandstand. All of us. And then everyone will come out to listen. Including the baker and his wife!'

'Fantastic!' yelled Mr Stamper. 'Then Pluck and Aggie can sneak into the bakery without anyone noticing. But... we've only got one trumpet between us. How can you give a concert with just one little trumpet?'

'Singing,' the oldest little Stamper said. 'We'll sing every song we know.'

The whole family climbed up onto the bandstand.

The little Stamper with a trumpet started blowing. It was nice and loud and it sounded very cheerful and a few passers-by stopped to listen.

And then the other Stampers started singing. They sang very beautifully. They sang *Baa, Baa, Black Sheep*. And the trumpet played along.

Now doors began opening all along the high street and people came out. The butcher left his shop unattended. And so did the grocer.

When the song was over, the Stampers started a new song. And by the third song, the baker and his wife had finally come out too.

They kept on singing. People loved it. A free Saturday morning concert on the bandstand... What a surprise.

And very cautiously, Pluck and Aggie snuck in through the back door of the bakery. And yep, there they were, six seagull eggs in a bowl. No... there were five of them, with a beautiful orange egg in with them.

Very carefully they picked up the eggs. A narrow lane led back to the tow truck. Aggie held the bowl on her lap.

And while the Stampers kept singing and playing music for their audience, Pluck sped back to the beach house.

Aggie put the bowl down on the floor. Then they opened the wardrobe.

Shirley flew out screeching with fury. But then she saw the eggs!

'My babies!' she cried. My dear little eggs! Are they still alive? Are they still warm?'

'They've been right next to the oven the whole time,' Aggie said. 'That kept them warm.'

Immediately Shirley sat on the eggs, but first she used her beak to quickly flick the orange egg out of the bowl.

'Why are you throwing that one out?' Aggie asked indignantly. 'Hatch that egg out too!'

'It's not my egg,' Shirley said. 'It's a cuckoo's egg. The egg of a sea cuckoo! You think I'm crazy? I'm not hatching out a sea cuckoo's egg.'

Then the Stamper family came home. When they saw Shirley sitting on the bowl they all cheered. 'Hooray! We did it! We did it!' they shouted. 'And we got a bag of toffees from the grocer. For singing so well.'

Carl with the wooden leg, who had flown to the village and back with them, came to look in on Shirley too and said, 'I'll go catch a nice fish for you, Shirl.' Nobody bothered about the orange egg. Nobody except Aggie, that is. She picked it up and wrapped it carefully in a woollen rag. Then she laid it in a warm spot in the kitchen near the stove.. *Maybe it will hatch out...* she thought. *I've never seen a sea cuckoo. I'm very curious.*

'Listen, everyone,' Mr Stamper said. 'One last thing. We need to give back the baker's bowl. With six ordinary chicken eggs. After all, he still has to make his egg custard.'

'He can have his bowl back in three weeks,' Shirley shrieked. 'I'm sitting on it now. I'm not getting off again!'

'We'll give you another bowl,' Mr Stamper said. 'One that's much prettier.'

'I don't want another bowl! I'm not getting off again!' Shirley screeched.

'Leave her,' Pluck said. 'She's still upset. Tomorrow we'll make a beautiful nest for her. Out on the porch.'

'No!' Shirley cried. 'I'm not going outside.'

'Fine, Shirley,' they all said soothingly. 'You just stay inside and hatch out your eggs. You don't have to do anything you don't want to.'

Pluck Goes Back

Shirley the seagull was on the porch. Her eggs were in a big red pan with sand in it. And she was sitting on them very happily and very patiently. Now and then her brother, Carl with the wooden leg, came by to say hello.

'How's it going?' Carl asked. 'You comfortable?'

'It's going well,' Shirley said. 'I'm very comfortable.'

'First you were sitting on a kind of dish,' Carl said. 'A big bowl. Why have you moved to a pan?'

'They had to take the bowl back to the baker,' Shirley said. 'They took it out from under me. I didn't want to change, but they said I had to. And then I got to choose what to put my nest in. And I chose the big saucepan.'

'That's right,' said Mr Stamper, who had come out onto the porch. 'Now we can't make any stews or soups. But that doesn't matter. We took the bowl back to the baker's. With six chicken eggs in it. We put it down in the shop when no one was looking.'

'Where's Pluck?' Carl asked. 'I've got a message for him.'

'Pluck's having a swim,' said Mr Stamper. 'With Aggie and all the little Stampers. But I think I hear them coming. Yep, here they are.'

All of the kids came home, sun-tanned and hungry.

And Carl said, 'Hello, Pluck. I went into town today. And I bumped into Dolly near the Pill Building. She said to say hello.'

'Thanks,' said Pluck. 'Is she ok? Is everything all right?'

'Hmmm...' said Carl.

'What do you mean, "Hmmm"? Has Dolly got some kind of problem?'

'She asked if you'd be coming home soon,' Carl said. 'She said there were difficulties.'

'What kind of difficulties? What's going on?'

'I don't know,' Carl said. 'She said you don't have to come back right away, but it

would be wonderful if you could think about heading home soon.'

'Oh,' said Pluck. 'I think I'd better go home straightaway then.'

Aggie and all of the little Stampers called out, 'No! Stay here!' And even Shirley looked up from her pan and moaned, 'Don't go!'

But Pluck grabbed his case. 'I've been here for a whole week now,' he said. 'It's time I went home and checked on Zaza.'

He climbed into his tow truck. After he had said goodbye and was about to drive off, Aggie came running out of the house with 'something' in a woollen rag. 'Can you take this with you, but very carefully?' she asked.

'What is it?'

'The sea cuckoo egg. Maybe you can get someone to hatch it out.'

'Give it to me,' Pluck said. 'I'll be very careful with it.'

'I've got something else too,' Aggie said. 'A letter to my mother. Could you give it to her?'

'Can I put it in the letterbox?' Pluck asked. 'Your mother's not that fond of me, you know. And I'm a bit scared of her.'

'Slip it in the letterbox then,' Aggie said.

With Aggie and the Stampers shouting and waving goodbye, Pluck drove off from Egham. He drove through the green fields without a care, because he knew the way. At least... he thought he knew the way. But after driving for an hour, he came to a T-junction. With a road sign. And all three directions said: EGHAM.

'Oh, no...' Pluck sighed. 'Which road do I take? All three of them go back to Egham. I must have taken a wrong turn after all. Which road shall I take... It doesn't really matter... They're all wrong.' Then he heard a very clear sound coming from the left side of his body: '*Tooo tooo...*'

Ah! Of course! He had his shell in his left pocket. The Tootenlisp.

He pulled out the shell and held it up to his ear.

At first he only heard a quiet rustling. But then the Tootenlisp's tiny voice said, 'Over the grath between the greenhoutheth.'

Pluck looked around. On his right were greenhouses. The Tootenlisp meant, 'Over the grass between the greenhouses.' Carefully Pluck drove up onto the grass. It was horribly bumpy and he had to go very slowly, but after half an hour he was back on a road he knew.

'Thanks a lot, Tootenlisp,' he said. And now it wasn't difficult at all. He drove straight to the city.

When he went into his room in the tower with his case, he found Zaza in a corner near the cupboard.

'Hello,' Pluck said. 'I'm back. How are you?'

'Hello,' Zaza said. 'I'm fine. But I'm glad you're home again.'

'I hear there are difficulties,' Pluck said. 'Dolly sent for me.'

'Difficulties?' said Zaza. 'I don't know anything about that. I don't have any difficulties. Apart from my apple peel. It's all dry and shrivelled.'

'I've got an apple in my pocket,' Pluck said. 'You can have the peel. And then I'll go look for Dolly.'

But no matter how much Pluck searched and whistled, Dolly didn't show up.

'And I really wanted to ask her if she knew someone for the egg,' Pluck said. 'It needs to be hatched out. And Dolly knows so many birds in the neighbourhood...'

Then he suddenly thought of Mrs Jeffrey. She lived on the seventh floor of the Pill Building. With Mr Jeffrey. And she had birds. All kinds of birds in cages.

Carrying the beautiful orange egg very

carefully, he rang Mrs Jeffrey's doorbell.

'Do you think one of your birds would hatch out a strange egg?' Pluck asked.

Mrs Jeffrey looked at the egg. 'I'm not sure any bird would want to hatch that one out,' she said.

'Wait a sec...' Mr Jeffrey said. 'I've got an idea. What if we did it ourselves?'

'You want to sit on an egg for three weeks?' Mrs Jeffrey asked.

'No... but we've got an electric blanket on our bed, haven't we? It's always nice and warm. If we put the egg under it... then move over to one side a little.'

'Yes, please,' Pluck said. 'I'll come back in about four weeks to ask what hatched out of the egg. Thank you, bye.'

'Wait a sec...' Mr Jeffrey said. 'You don't happen to know what kind of egg it is, do you?'

'It's a sea cuckoo egg,' said Pluck.

'A sea cuckoo?' said Mr Jeffrey. 'Nonsense. No such thing.'

'That's what they told me,' Pluck said.

'Well, never mind,' said Mrs Jeffrey. 'Whatever kind of egg it is, a bird will hatch out of it. We're very curious. Bye, Pluck.'

Pluck went off in search of Dolly. But Dolly was nowhere to be found.

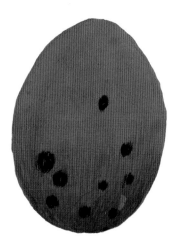

Dovey Gardens

Pluck had come home from Egham-on-Sea. He was back in his tower with Zaza. But he couldn't find Dolly anywhere and that was horrible. Because it was Dolly the pigeon who had sent him a message that he had to come back.

'Have you looked everywhere?' Zaza asked.

'Everywhere,' Pluck said. 'On the roof and out on the street. And in the park. I stood under the oak tree Dolly lives in. I called and whistled but there was no sign of her.'

'Did you go to Mr Penn's shop too?'

'Of course. Mr Penn doesn't know where she is either. He was a bit worried, because usually she flies in for a quick visit at least once a day.'

'Maybe she's gone to stay with someone,' Zaza said. 'Her family or something like that.'

'She doesn't have a family,' Pluck said. 'But hang on... you've given me an idea. Dovey Gardens!'

Pluck jumped up, grabbed his cap and ran to the door.

'Hey, where you going?' Zaza asked. 'Where on earth is Dovey Gardens?'

'You know,' Pluck said. 'At the back of the park. That big stretch of forest. Real wild, un-touched forest...'

'No, I don't know,' Zaza said. 'I stay away from forests. Cockroaches aren't woodland creatures. They're indoor creatures.'

'OK,' Pluck said. 'I'll explain it to you. It used to be a garden, a great big garden with tall trees. But that garden has gone wild: there are bushes everywhere and the pond has turned into a frog pool. Lots of turtledoves live in the trees. Grown-ups never go there, but kids do. We play cops and robbers there. It's a great place to play.'

'And the turtledoves are related to Dolly?' Zaza asked.

'Exactly. They're cousins. That's why I'm going there to see if she's there. Bye, see you later.'

'Shouldn't you take that letter on the table?' Zaza asked.

'What letter? Oh, that's right. The letter Aggie gave me! For her mother.'

'You should have delivered it ages ago.'

'I know,' Pluck said. 'It's just... I'm a bit scared of Mrs Brightner. I'll go and put it in her letterbox.'

But when Pluck went to Aggie's flat to look for the letterbox, the window opened and Mrs Brightner poked her head out.

'Who are you again?' she asked.

'I'm Pluck. I'm here with a letter from your daughter, Aggie. From Egham.'

'Thank you, you can give it straight to me.'

Mrs Brightner took the letter and Pluck was about to walk off, when she said, 'So you were there too. In the beach house with the Stamper family.'

'Yes, Mrs Brightner,' Pluck said. 'It was great.'

'Lovely,' said Mrs Brightner. 'Aggie says here in her letter that she's enjoying herself. And she'll be staying away for a few more weeks. That's convenient, because I'm having a big clean up. I hope she's not getting dirty there in Egham?'

'Oh, no,' Pluck said. 'You can't get dirty on a beach.'

'Of course you can get dirty on a beach,' said Mrs Brightner. 'With all that filthy sand and all that filthy seawater. By the way, did you see that all kinds of things are going to happen in the park?'

'In the park? I haven't seen anything,' Pluck said. 'What's going to happen?'

'They're going to clear Dovey Gardens,' said Mrs Brightner cheerfully.

'They're going to clear it?'

'Yes, they're going to cut down all the trees and pull out all the weeds and bushes and plants. And they're going to pave it. They're going to turn it into a Paved Square. With neat, tidy flower beds in the middle.'

Pluck was shocked. Dovey Gardens was going to disappear... with all those magnificent trees.

'Haven't you seen the hut at the entrance to the park?' Mrs Brightner asked.

'I did see a small wooden building,' Pluck said.

'That's the Park Master's hut. He's in

charge of getting rid of all that dirty rubbish. Clearing away that messy forest. You should go and have a look. And thanks for dropping off the letter.'

Pluck left. He went straight to the park. The hut was next to the entrance and Pluck could look in through the open door.

There was the Park Master, sitting at a desk that was covered with papers and talking on the phone. This was where they were making plans to chop down that beautiful forest.

Feeling very sad, Pluck walked further into the park. Behind the great big oak tree was the start of a winding path that was almost completely overgrown with tall grass, weeds and branches. This was the path that led to Dovey Gardens.

Squeezing in through the bushes, Pluck thought, *Now I understand why Dolly sent for me. She must have heard about it too. I think this is where I'll find her.*

He was now standing in a clearing surrounded by rustling trees. Ferns and moss were growing there. There were crickets and bees. Birds were singing on the branches above him, but he couldn't see Dolly.

It was so quiet here and so beautiful. And it was all going to disappear. Just imagine... they

were going to lay paving stones here... and gravel.

Pluck went to sit down in the grass for a moment, but suddenly heard a voice under him shout out in fright, 'Hey, careful!'

He jumped back up and looked down. Standing in front of him was a mouse. A field mouse with frightened, tiny little eyes and trembling whiskers.

'You almost sat on my family,' the mouse shouted accusingly.

'Sorry,' Pluck said. 'I didn't see them. Where are they?'

'Here,' the mouse said. 'Next to the tree root.'

Pluck bent down to look. There, between the dry leaves and grass, he saw the mouse's nest. There was a mother mouse and seven bald baby mice.

'Oh, cute,' Pluck said.

'Yes, very cute,' said the father mouse. 'And you almost sat on them.'

'I'll be more careful in the future,' Pluck said.

'Good,' said the mouse. 'And now you're here, tell me if it's true that they're going to cut down this forest. Please tell me it's not true!'

'I'm sorry, but I'm afraid it really is true,' said Pluck.

'And where are we supposed to live?' asked the mouse. 'Where can I go with a wife and seven bald babies?'

'I don't know...' Pluck sighed. 'If you have to, I can help you move.'

'Move?' the mouse exclaimed. 'Where?'

Just then something fluttered down into the green grass. Something white. It was Dolly the pigeon.

'Have you heard?' she cried. 'We have to think of something. We have to stop them!'

The Park Master

They were having a big meeting in Dovey Gardens. Pluck was in the middle and sitting around him were Dolly and father mouse and three turtledoves, cousins of Dolly's. There was also a hedgehog and a very jumpy rabbit.

'Tell us, quick,' said Dolly. 'When do they start? When are they going to cut down the forest?'

'I don't know,' Pluck said. 'I just heard from Mrs Brightner that they're planning to clear Dovey Gardens. And I know that the Park Master has a wooden office at the park entrance. He's got all kinds of papers there: plans and drawings. It probably says on those papers.'

'Eek!' gasped the jumpy rabbit. 'I heard something!'

All of the animals started and looked fear-fully in all directions. Pluck was up on his feet and looking around. But there was nothing. Just the chirping of crickets.

'What did you hear?' Dolly asked.

'Nothing… I think…' said the jumpy rabbit. 'I'm just so nervous. I keep hearing things.'

'We're scared enough already without you making it worse,' the father mouse grumbled. 'We're safe here for now. Can't you go and talk to the Park Master, Pluck?'

'Yeah,' said the hedgehog, 'and make sure he stays away from Dovey Gardens.'

'But how?' Pluck asked. 'How could I do that?'

'You're so big and strong,' the hedgehog said. 'Yes,' said all the other animals, 'that's right. Pluck is big and strong. He can stop the Park Master.'

'Rubbish,' Pluck said. 'The Park Master is a lot bigger and stronger than I am. No, we'll have to come up with a trick. But I can't think of any.'

'Let's all think,' said one of the turtledoves.

They sat there in a circle in complete silence, trying to think. And then suddenly the rabbit shouted, 'Help!' jumping up in the air in fright.

'What is it? What is it?' everyone cried fearfully. And they looked around, but they couldn't see anything.

'I thought I saw something…' the rabbit blurted. But there was nothing there.

'Stop it!' shouted Pluck, who'd had the biggest shock of all. He was up on his feet

again and now he paced to and fro impatiently trying to think.

'Careful! You'll fall in the pool!' Dolly warned him. Pluck jumped back just in time. The pool was green and muddy. If you didn't look closely, you couldn't even tell it was water.

'You know what,' Pluck said. 'I'll go see the Park Master. I'll ask him to leave Dovey Gardens alone.'

'Right!' 'Yes!' 'Hooray!' the animals shouted.

And so, ten minutes later, Pluck stepped into the Park Master's office.

The Park Master was busy drawing up a large plan. It was the plan for Dovey Gardens and it showed exactly what it was going to look like. When Pluck walked in, he said, 'Can't you knock?'

'The door was open,' said Pluck.

'You should still knock first,' said the Park Master. 'What do you want?'

'I've heard you're going to cut down Dovey Gardens,' Pluck said.

'That's right,' the Park Master said, rubbing his hands. 'It's going to be beautiful. You can see it on this drawing. Come closer and I'll show you.'

Pluck took a step closer. The Park Master pointed at the different parts of the plan he was drawing.

'See...' he said, 'here there's a big filthy puddle, we're going to fill that with concrete. And we're going to lay hundreds of paving stones all around it. Then we'll cut down the trees and turn it into an enormous paved square. Here...' he pointed with a thumb, 'here there's going to be a car park. That'll be paved too. And this will be a gravel path. And here, we'll put two stone benches to sit on. And this – see this circle? That's going to be a flowerbed with a wrought-iron fence around it.'

'That's horrible!' Pluck cried.

The Park Master's mouth dropped. 'What did you say?' he asked.

'I mean...' Pluck spluttered. 'I mean, it's horrible to lose those beautiful trees. And all the plants. It's so lovely and peaceful there.'

'Oh, it will still be peaceful,' the Park Master said. 'We're going to hang up big signs saying, NO NOISE. And whenever anyone feels like it, they can lie down on the stone benches for a nap. And once a year, on Easter Monday, all the children can come and roller-skate on the paving stones. Won't that be fantastic? Well, what do you think?'

Pluck summoned up all his courage and said, 'Mr Park Master, sir, I've actually come to ask if you could please leave this bit of forest. I mean, leave it as it is. You see, a lot of animals live there.'

'Animals?' the Park Master said. 'I've never seen any animals. What kind of animals?'

'Birds,' said Pluck. 'And crickets and frogs.'

The Park Master stared at him in astonishment. 'Is that all?' he asked.

'There's a family of mice too,' said Pluck. 'A father mouse and a mother mouse and seven tiny little baby mice.'

Now the Park Master started to laugh so hard his wooden hut began to shake. 'Ha-ha-ha!' he roared. 'Mice! Shall I tear up my beautiful plan then? Because there are mice living there? Ha-ha-ha!'

Pluck got angry. 'There's nothing funny about it,' he shouted. 'It's not just mice. There are hedgehogs too with baby hedgehogs. And rabbits. And lots of turtledoves. And lots more. And have you ever seen how beautiful it is?'

'Beautiful?' the Park Master said. 'I think it's messy. No, my boy, I'm very sorry, but it can't be helped. The bulldozer arrives the day after tomorrow. And an electric saw to cut the trees. It's bad luck for the mice...' And at the word 'mice', the Park Master started to laugh again.

'So... it starts the day after tomorrow?' Pluck asked.

'Yes, my boy. And you'll see. It will be beautiful. I'm going there a bit later... to Dovey Gardens. I need to make sure I've drawn it up right. There's something I need to measure too. Goodbye.'

A very unhappy Pluck stepped out of the hut.

When he arrived back at Dovey Gardens,

all the animals were waiting for him next to the pool.

'And? How did it turn out?' they asked.

'Very badly,' Pluck said. 'It's going to happen the day after tomorrow.'

'Didn't you tell him how many animals live here? And how many baby animals?'

'I told him, but he just laughed.'

'What a nasty man!'

'What a horrible man!' cried the father mouse.

'He's coming here later,' Pluck said. 'He said there were a few things he had to measure.'

The Spray Can

The Park Master parked his car next to the pond in the park. He got out and took the narrow path to Dovey Gardens. In one hand he was holding a big sheet of paper, in the other a yardstick. Bent over and sighing from the effort, he squeezed under the overhanging branches. It took him a long time because the path was overgrown with thorn bushes. And he was a fat Park Master.

But finally he made it to the open space next to the green frog pool in the middle of Dovey Gardens.

It was very quiet. No birds were singing, the crickets were silent and the frogs had stopped croaking. It was as if all the animals had fled, but they hadn't. They were hiding.

Pluck was sitting behind a bush with Dolly. And with them were three turtledoves, cousins of Dolly's, and the father mouse and the rabbit, who kept jumping up nervously and rustling the leaves.

'Stay still...' Dolly whispered. 'You too, Pluck, stop fidgeting.'

'Why do we have to stay still?' Pluck whispered back. 'Why is everyone hiding?'

'Shhh...'

'He's only coming to have a look...' Pluck went on. 'He's not going to do anything.'

'Shhh...' Dolly said again. 'Just watch. Something's going to happen.'

'What?'

'You'll see.'

The Park Master was right in front of them. He looked around with satisfaction. This whole forest was going to disappear. All the trees and all the bushes... They were going to cut everything down. They would turn it into a neat and tidy square with nothing but paving stones. He took the big piece of paper and peered at it. It was his drawing, the plan with all the little circles and dots that showed just what they were going to do. This was where the gravel path would come and the stone benches would come over there... It was all perfect, he just had to measure one last thing.

'Nothing's happening...' Pluck whispered.

'Wait...' Dolly said. 'The moment he walks past the elderberry.'

'What's there?'

Dolly fell silent. But the father mouse continued. 'The bees...' he said, 'there's a beehive behind there, remember?'

'We've arranged for the bees to attack...' said one of the turtledoves.

Then the Park Master walked past the elderberry.

First it was just one or two angry bees zooming around his head. He lashed out at them with the big sheet of paper, but all at once he was surrounded by at least a hundred big brown buzzing bees.

The Park Master stood his ground, swatting at the bees, flapping the piece of paper and swearing under his breath, until one of them stung him on the nose. He screamed at the top of his lungs and ran back the way he'd come. He had to push the

branches out of the way and keep the swarming bees off at the same time. There were a lot more than a hundred by now and they were mean and menacing and chased him all the way back to his car, buzzing around until he was inside panting with the windows shut.

Dovey Gardens wasn't quiet now. The birds were singing like crazy, the turtledoves were cooing, the crickets were chirping and the frogs in the pool were croaking very loudly.

'It worked!' Dolly cried, fluttering around excitedly. 'He's gone!'

'Gone forever!' cheered the mouse. 'He'll never dare to come back now.'

The only one who wasn't cheering was Pluck.

'What are you getting up for? Where are you going?' Dolly asked.

'I'm going to see Mr Penn to ask his advice,' Pluck said. 'I don't think this is going to make any difference. He won't let a swarm of bees chase him off forever. He'll come back with men and a bulldozer. You'll see!'

And while Dovey Gardens celebrated, Pluck climbed into his truck and drove to the Pill Building.

When he was halfway there, he saw a lady standing by the side of the road. It was Mrs Brightner, who waved him down.

'Could you give me a lift?' she asked. 'I'm in such a rush.'

'Sure,' Pluck said. 'Climb in.'

He pulled up in front of the Pill Building to drop her off and as she was getting out of the truck she said, 'You see, I have to get my spray can as fast as I can. The Park Master was stung by bees in Dovey Gardens. I'll teach those bees a lesson!'

And before Pluck could say anything in reply, she went inside.

'That's horrible...' Pluck mumbled and he drove back to Dovey Gardens at top speed to warn his friends. Especially the insects, they were in great danger!

Fortunately it took Mrs Brightner ages to get there.

She'd brought her spray can. She had to force her way through the bushes and when she finally reached the open spot next to the frog pool, it was silent and deserted again. Butterflies and crickets and beetles... everything that had wings... wasps and bees and ladybirds... they'd all flown off to safety. The ants and worms and spiders had crept down into holes and dark corners.

There weren't any insects anywhere.

Oh, yes there was... high above the frog pool, a big solitary bee was dancing in the air.

'You little monster!' Mrs Brightner cried. 'You wait. I'll get you!'

She took three big steps forward and splash! She was lying in the pool. She hadn't even seen that it was water... With all that duckweed on it, it looked like a nice little meadow.

Mrs Brightner had fallen face first into the pool. Dirty water splashed in all directions... croaking frogs jumped out of the way as she sniffed and spat her way back up onto dry land.

The spray can was still in the pool.

Pluck was hiding behind the bushes with Dolly and the other animals. They had all seen it happen and Pluck was the only one who felt sorry for the poor lady.

'Shall I go after her?' he asked. 'To give her a ride home.'

'Don't do that,' Dolly said. 'She'll be furious if she sees you.'

Meanwhile Mrs Brightner was on her way home. She hurried through the park, sopping wet and green all over. There was a bunch of water lilies on her hat and she looked like a big, wet, green toad.

When she walked into the Pill Building lobby, she left big green footprints on the beautiful marble floor. The doorman stopped her. He didn't recognise her and snapped, 'Hey, you! Where do you think you're going?'

'Let me through!' Mrs Brightner shouted. 'I need to get in the lift.'

The doorman was about to say, 'Toads aren't allowed...' but Mrs Brightner wiped the duckweed off her face and he recognised her.

'Goodness... I beg your pardon, Mrs Brightner...' he cried. 'What happened?' But she ignored his question and stepped into the lift.

There were already three ladies and a gentleman in the lift and when Mrs Brightner sloshed in to join them, they squeezed together in the far corner to avoid touching her.

Silently they went up in the lift. And when Mrs Brightner got out at her own floor, the three ladies said to the gentleman, 'Wasn't that Mrs Brightner?'

'Indeed it was,' said the gentleman.

'How is it possible?' the ladies said. 'She's usually so respectable! Just look at that... she left a big puddle on the floor of the lift.'

Dolly Does Something

Pluck and Dolly were in the bookshop talking to Mr Penn. All three of them looked very unhappy. And that was hardly surprising.

'So they already have a bulldozer in the park?' asked Mr Penn.

'An enormous bulldozer,' said Pluck.

'And a truck with a giant saw,' said Dolly.

'And big stacks of paving stones...' Pluck added gloomily. 'And piles of gravel. All next to the path to Dovey Gardens.'

'Do you have any idea when they plan to start work?' Mr Penn asked.

'No,' said Pluck.

'Have the workers started to get things ready?'

'We haven't seen any workers yet. Just monstrous big machines.'

'And we were so happy...' Dolly moaned. 'We thought the bees had chased the Park Master away forever. The whole forest was celebrating. We all thought the plan was off. And now it's going ahead after all.'

'I knew it wouldn't help,' Pluck said. 'People are stronger than birds and bees. Can't you think of anything, Mr Penn?'

'I've been racking my brains for days,' Mr Penn said. 'And yesterday I went to talk to the Park Master. In his office.'

'I suppose that didn't help either,' Pluck said.

'No. I told him it would be such a shame to cut down those beautiful trees. And a pity to lose that wild nature reserve... but he said paving stones look better than weeds.'

'Didn't you tell him it was home to lots of animals?' Dolly cried. 'Families of mice with loads of little babies? Turtledoves that will lose their nests and frogs that need water to live in?'

'Ah...' Pluck sighed, 'I already told him that. He just laughed. He thinks it's ridiculous to get wound up about baby mice.'

'All he cares about is his beautiful plan,' Mr Penn said. 'He sits there in his office in that hut adding lines and circles to that big drawing of his. Do you know the one I mean? The big drawing of Dovey Gardens and how they're going to turn it into a square.'

'Open the door, will you?' Dolly exclaimed suddenly. 'Let me out...'

Pluck opened the door for her. 'Where are you going?' he asked. But she was already gone.

Mr Penn was sitting there thinking with his face in his hands. 'I know!' he shouted... and all of a sudden there was a happy glint in his eyes.

'What?' Pluck asked. 'What?'

'No, maybe not...' Mr Penn said. 'It's too late now... we don't have time.'

'What did you think of?' Pluck asked.

'No, no...' Mr Penn lamented. 'The bulldozer's already there and all that other stuff too. They'll start tomorrow morning of course.'

'But what did you want to do?' Pluck asked.

'I have a friend,' Mr Penn said. 'A good

friend who would almost certainly be willing to help us.'

'Can't you phone him?'

'No, he doesn't have a telephone.'

'Can I go see him?' Pluck asked. 'I've got my truck.'

'It's much too far,' Mr Penn said. 'It's miles away. In Hasselworth.'

'I'm sure I can drive all the way to Hasselworth...' Pluck said.

'It's a whole day's drive...' Mr Penn said gloomily. 'And a whole day back again. If not more, because your truck doesn't go that fast... It's too late!'

'I can still try!' Pluck cried. 'Maybe I'll be back in time...'

The shop door opened and the Park Master came in, flapping a big sheet of paper. He was very upset. He was furious. 'I need a large sheet of graph paper immediately!' he snarled.

'Of course, sir,' Mr Penn said politely. 'Just sit down, I'll show you what I have.'

'It's a disgrace!' the Park Master shouted angrily.

'Has something bad happened?' Pluck asked.

'You're asking me if something bad has happened? You can say that again! Look at this! Look at the plan I've been working on for months. My drawing of the new Dovey Gardens. Completely ruined.'

He laid the drawing flat on the counter. It was dirty. In fact, it was filthy.

'Oh...' said Mr Penn. 'How did that happen?'

'A pigeon!' the Park Master screamed. 'Have you ever heard of anything so outrageous? I'm sitting there quietly in my office. In that wooden hut in the park. You know the one I mean? Well, I'm sitting there hard at work on this drawing. Being as neat and tidy

as I possibly can and you know what happens? A pigeon flies in. Do you believe it?'

'Tsk,' said Mr Penn, shaking his head indignantly.

'The creature flies straight to my desk...' the Park Master continued. 'And what does it do? It... um –' The Park Master restrained himself just in time.

'Sorry,' he said. 'I almost said a very rude word. But perhaps you understand what I mean, Mr Penn.'

'I understand,' said Mr Penn. 'In fact, I can see it. What that creature did, I mean. Do you have to start all over again?'

'Not entirely,' said the Park Master. 'It's not that bad, thank goodness. But it will put me back at least two days. We were supposed to start first thing tomorrow morning. The bulldozer is already there. Everything's ready. Now we're going to have to start two days later. Do you have that paper or not? Where is it?'

'I'm terribly sorry,' Mr Penn said in a friendly voice. 'As it happens I'm completely out of graph paper. I don't have any left at all.'

'Just what I needed...' the Park Master groaned. 'Now I have to go into town to find the right paper.' And grumbling angrily he walked out of the shop.

Mr Penn and Pluck looked at each other.

'That was clever of Dolly,' said Mr Penn.

'Fantastic,' Pluck said. 'That gives us two

111

extra days! Now I can go to Hasselworth. To see that friend of yours. What's his name? And where does he live?'

'It's on the other side of the River Haze,' Mr Penn said. 'You have to cross the river on the big ferry. Then you head east.'

'And what's his name? Who am I looking for?'

'Well, he doesn't actually have a name,' Mr Penn said. 'He's a hermite.'

'What a funny word,' Pluck said. 'I always thought it was hermit. With an IT on the end.'

'This one's a hermite,' Mr Penn said. 'And I'm not sure where exactly he lives. He keeps a very low profile.'

And now Dolly flew in. 'How was it?' she shouted proudly.

'Magnificent,' said Mr Penn. 'How did you manage it? So much!'

The Ferry

Very early in the morning, Pluck began driving south to the River Haze. He had to cross the river. The hermite lived somewhere on the other side.

It was a very long trip and Pluck had twenty-four sandwiches with him in the tow truck in plastic bags. And two cartons of milk and a big bag of sweets. Mr Penn had told him how to get there. 'Don't take the main road,' he said. 'That's much too busy and,

anyway, it's better to take the back roads, that's shorter. Be careful and watch out and don't drive too fast!'

Pluck didn't drive too fast, but he tried to make the best time he could because it was urgent. He had two days. It was now Tuesday morning and in two days, on Thursday morning, they were going to start. That was when men would come to destroy Dovey Gardens with their bulldozer. They would cut down

the trees and chase away the birds and murder the little baby mice and destroy the whole forest. 'The hermite is the only one who can help us,' Mr Penn had said.

It was a beautiful summer's day and the narrow back roads weren't busy at all. In his left pocket, Pluck had the shell, the Tootenlisp. That made him feel very safe: if he got lost, the Tootenlisp could tell him the way. But so far it had been easy and Pluck ate four peanut-butter sandwiches while driving along.

But then it began. It started to get foggy. At first it was just a few wisps of mist over the fields.

And then it got thicker and thicker. Pluck kept driving, but he had to go a lot slower because he could only see a little bit of the road.

If it stays like this, it will take me two days just to get there, he thought sadly. *It's almost midday already and I'm hardly making any progress.*

But then he came to a sign. The fog was so thick he had to get out of the truck and go up close to read what was written on it.

FERRY 1 m, the sign said.

Pluck sighed with relief. *One mile isn't far. I'm close to the river and close to the ferry. Now I just have to hope the ferry's on this side and doesn't leave just when I get there.*

He drove as fast as he dared. And after a few minutes he saw an enormous shape looming in front of him in the grey fog. It had to be the ferry.

But there weren't any other cars at all and no bikes and no motorbikes. There weren't even any pedestrians waiting to board the ferry.

Pluck got out and walked up to the ferry. Now he could see the river, at least a little bit of it. The enormous boat was moored next to the bank.

It was completely empty. There was no one in sight. Oh, yes there was... there was a man working on the upper deck.

'Hello!' Pluck yelled.

The man looked down at him.

'When does the ferry go!' Pluck called.

The man shook his head. 'It's not running!' he called down. 'Because of the fog!!'

The ferry wasn't running because of the fog... of course... he should have thought of that before... ferries don't run in such thick fog.

But what now? How was he supposed to cross the river? Wait for the fog to clear? That could take all day.

Pluck looked at the water splashing against the bank and for a moment he thought of swimming. He was a very good swimmer...

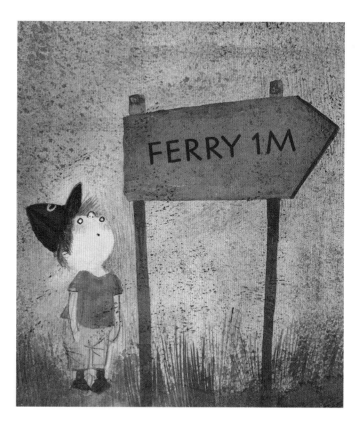

but... No, it was nonsense. You can't swim across such a wide river, you'd be swept away by the current.

Then Pluck heard something on his left, '*Toooo-toooo.*'

The Tootenlisp!

He pulled the shell out of his pocket and held it up to his ear.

'Go left,' the shell said. 'Between thothe two houtheth.'

'Between those two houses over there?'

'Yeth.'

Pluck climbed in and drove between the two small houses. It was a narrow bumpy little path and he felt like he was driving away from the river.

'Are you sure, Tootenlisp?' he asked. 'I'm getting further and further away from the river.'

'I'm never mithtaken,' said the shell.

It seemed as if the windy path would never end, but suddenly he saw reeds. Tall reeds. The path had looped back to the river.

'Thtop,' said the Tootenlisp. 'Thereth a crothing here.'

'A what? Oh, a crossing.'

Pluck got out of his truck and walked through the tall reeds looking for a boat. But he couldn't see any boats anywhere.

'There's nothing here,' he said, holding the shell up to his ear. 'No ferry, no ferryman, no boat, no crossing.'

'There mutht be,' said the shell.

Pluck decided to walk along the riverbank a little.

The fog was still so thick that you could only see a few feet in front of your nose. And

that was why he suddenly found himself right in front of a big houseboat he hadn't even noticed. There were steps up to the front door and Pluck knocked on it. A lady opened the door and asked what he wanted. 'There's supposed to be a ferry here somewhere,' Pluck said. 'A crossing. I have to get to the other side of the river.'

'You have to take the big ferry, son,' the lady said.

'It's not running,' Pluck said. 'Because of the fog. But I heard that there's another one here, a little one. Maybe a ferryman with a rowing boat.'

'No,' the lady said. 'Not around here. Maybe there used to be... a long time ago... but not anymore.' And she closed the door.

Pluck walked back to his truck sadly. He sat down on the driver's seat and thought. What should he do now? There was no ferry here. And suddenly he got very angry at the Tootenlisp for leading him in the wrong direction. It had let him down.

He took the shell out of his pocket and said reproachfully. 'You *did* make a mistake. There's no ferry here!'

The shell rustled for a moment, then said very quietly, 'Thorry.'

Pluck put it back in his pocket. What use was a shell that told him to go in the wrong direction? And then said 'sorry' when things went wrong? 'I'll have to wait for the fog to clear,' Pluck said. 'There's nothing else I can do.'

He started on the next bag of sandwiches. Meat paste.

The Old Fisherman

Pluck stood in the fog next to his truck on a narrow path along the river. It was late in the afternoon and there was no sign of the fog lifting.

'I'll just have to drive back to the big ferry,' Pluck said to himself. 'And wait there until it starts running again.'

He managed to turn the tow truck around and was about to drive off when he heard the reeds rustling.

A boat perhaps...

Pluck got out and parted the tall reeds on the bank of the river.

Sitting there by the water was a fisherman. An old man in the fog.

'You don't happen to know if there's a ferry here, do you?' Pluck asked.

'A ferry?'

'Yes, a boat that goes back and forth,' Pluck said. 'A ferryboat. A crossing. I have to get to the other side.'

'There's a big ferry downstream a little,' the old fisherman said.

'Yes, I know. It's not running because of the fog. But I heard there's a ferryman here too.'

'Who told you that?'

For a moment Pluck didn't answer. He'd been about to say, 'My Tootenlisp.' But who would believe him if he told them that he had a shell that gave him directions?

That was why he just shrugged and said, 'Well... people. But they must have been mistaken. Thank you.'

He was about to go back to his truck, but the fisherman gestured for him to come closer. When Pluck was standing right next to him, he whispered, 'There is a boat.'

'Here?'

'There,' the man pointed. A few yards further along Pluck saw a rickety old driftwood construction. A landing place.

'I don't see a boat,' Pluck said. 'Will it come later, do you think?'

The fisherman gave him a frightened look.

'I wouldn't advise you to take that boat,' he said.

He was whispering as if he was scared someone might hear him. Even though they were the only people near and far, on the side of a mighty river in the thick grey fog.

'Why not? Does the boat leak or something?' Pluck asked.

'It doesn't leak,' the man said.

'Could I go on it with my truck? I've still got a long way to drive on the other side.'

'Your truck could go on it,' the fisherman said. 'It would fit. But I still wouldn't do it.'

'But why not?' Pluck was starting to get a little impatient. He was in a hurry and all he wanted to do was cross the river. And this man said there was a chance he could do just that.

'Could I call the ferryman, do you think?' he asked.

'Yes,' the old man said. 'Definitely. You could do that.'

'Do I just shout across the river?' Pluck asked. 'At the top of my voice?'

'No,' the fisherman said. 'No... I've heard you have to whistle. Three times on your fingers. Can you do that?'

'Sure,' Pluck said. He put two fingers in his mouth, but the old fisherman cried in terror, 'Wait... don't... not yet.'

He stood up, reeled in his line and started packing his things.

'You have to wait till I'm gone,' he said nervously. 'Promise you'll wait five minutes, until I've got a good distance away.' He had all his fishing gear in a bucket and started to hurry off through the reeds.

'At least tell me what's going on,' Pluck said. 'Don't leave without telling me what's so dangerous. You said the boat doesn't leak. Is the ferryman a bit scary?'

'You're not going to whistle before I've got a good distance away?' the old man asked in a trembling voice.

'No, I promise. But I'd like to know why you're so scared.'

'I don't like him,' the man said. 'Oh no, I don't care for him at all.'

'Why not? Isn't he a good ferryman? Do you see him sometimes?'

'I've never seen him,' the fisherman said. 'But my father told me all about him. *He* saw him once.'

'And?' Pluck asked. By now he was really very curious. And a little scared.

The fisherman looked around to make sure no one was listening. Then he said, 'The ferryman isn't a man.'

'No? What is he then? A woman?'

'No,' the fisherman said. He waved for Pluck to come closer and then, when he was standing right next to him, he whispered, 'He's a werewolf'.'

'What's a werewolf?' Pluck asked.

Now the fisherman hesitated. He didn't really know what a werewolf was either.

'Is it some kind of wolf?' Pluck asked.

'I've never seen him,' the old man said. 'But I know he's extremely dangerous. So very dangerous.'

'Does he eat people?' Pluck asked. 'Has he ever eaten anyone around here?'

The man had to think about that for a very long time. Then he shook his head. 'No,' he said. 'Not as far as I know.'

'Oh,' said Pluck.

'But that's because no one ever goes on his boat,' the man said. 'Everyone stays well away. You've been warned.'

Now the old fisherman really did go, leaving Pluck alone. He waited five minutes, just as he'd promised. Now he had to whistle on his fingers three times and the ferryman would come. The ferryman who was a werewolf. Pluck felt his heart pounding in his chest. He stepped out onto the wooden landing. And now he saw a post with a small wooden sign. The letters on it were almost gone from being out in the wind and the rain.

Pluck bent down and read:

TELL ME WHERE-WOLF
WHISTLE 3 X

Do I dare? He raised two fingers to his lips, but didn't whistle. Then he thought of his Tootenlisp. The shell had given him good directions all along. It hadn't made any mistakes, there *was* a crossing. Even if it was a very strange one.

What does a werewolf look like?

But... Pluck thought, *a tell-me-where wolf isn't actually the same as a werewolf.* He decided to consult the shell.

'Should I do it, Tootenlisp?' he asked, holding the shell up to his ear. The Tootenlisp remained silent. There wasn't any sound coming out of it at all. Not even a rustling sound. It was just an empty, hollow shell.

I think the Tootenlisp is offended... Pluck thought. *It's my own fault...*

The Tell Me Where-Wolf

Pluck had never been so alone. He was still standing on the wooden landing on the river in the thick fog. There was nobody around. Even the Tootenlisp had stopped talking to him. It wasn't even rustling anymore.

'It's time for me to think very clearly,' Pluck told himself.

'If I whistle three times, a ferryboat will come to take me across the river. But the ferryman's a wolf... a "where-wolf". So I won't do it. It would be really stupid to whistle. I'll just go back. I'll drive back along the river to the big ferry and wait for the fog to clear. Of course, that could take a very long time... It could take days. And then it'll be too late. It will be no use anymore... I have to cross the river now! Today! But I'm too scared to whistle. Oh, if only there was someone else here. Then I'd feel braver... Right now my heart has sunk into my boots...'

Pluck stared down at his boots, which looked the same as ever.

'Come on,' he said to himself. 'Decide! Either leave or whistle and call the wolf. Is a wolf something I should be scared of? All the animals I've ever met have been nice to me. And if it's too creepy... I'll run to my truck and drive off.'

Pluck put his fingers in his mouth and whistled. The shrill noise cut through the silence. Again and again... He whistled three times.

'There. Now I just stand here and try to be brave.'

For quite a while nothing happened. Pluck stood on the landing with his knees shaking and his heart pounding. The fog was so thick he could only see a little bit of grey water close to the bank. Then he heard the splash of oars.

He bravely held his ground. And then he saw something looming up. Quite close... A boat. A big flat boat. And on that boat, a shadowy figure was pulling on the oars. It was the ferryman.

He was a wolf. A very big wolf with a sou'wester and an oilskin. Pluck saw his shaggy jaws and was about to turn and run to his truck, when the wolf spoke. His voice wasn't the least bit frightening. It was hoarse and grumbling, but soft and a little shy. 'It must be a mistake, huh?' the wolf asked. 'You whistled by accident, didn't you?'

'No,' Pluck said, pointing to the small sign on the landing. 'It says here "whistle 3x". So I whistled three times. I'd like to cross over.'

'It can't be true,' said the wolf, shaking his shaggy head. 'You're fibbing.'

Pluck got a bit annoyed. 'I'm not fibbing,' he said. 'I'm in a hurry and I have to get to the other side of the river. I can bring my truck, can't I?'

'A truck,' the wolf gasped. 'It can't be true... I don't believe it.'

'It's true,' Pluck said. 'I'll just get my truck. Please don't go away.'

Pluck climbed into his tow truck and drove carefully onto the boat, which the wolf had moored with the flat end up against the landing.

'Right,' he said. 'Now row.'

The wolf tried to say something, but wasn't able to get it out. He was crying. Big fat tears streamed down his hairy face.

'What's wrong?' Pluck asked. 'Why are you crying?'

'It's... boo-hoo-hoo... ugh-ugh-ugh...' the wolf sobbed, 'ten long years...'

'What? What are you saying?'

'It's been ten long years!'

'What's been ten long years?'

The wolf wiped the tears off his face and sniffed loudly.

'It's been ten long years and no one's been on my ferry,' he said. 'I've waited ten years. But I'm a good ferryman. Now and then I take animals from one side to the other. A family of rats. Not so long ago, a foal that couldn't find its mother. A hare now and then. But people don't get on my boat. And that was why I was crying. I was crying for joy!'

'OK, but let's get going, shall we?' Pluck said. 'I'm in a terrible hurry, you know.'

'Oh, yes, of course!' the wolf said. 'We're leaving. Imagine... a real person on my boat. A person with a truck. A tow truck! Incredible.'

The wolf jumped up and down, making the boat rock dangerously. 'Hooray!' he shouted. 'Fantastic! Party time!'

'Stop...' Pluck said. 'Just row.'

'Don't worry. It's all sorted. We're on our way,' the wolf said.

He spat on his paws and started rowing with all his strength.

'Where would you like to go?' he asked. 'Just tell me where. I can take you all the way to the sea, if you like.'

'No, I don't want to go to the sea. I just have to get to the other side of the river.'

'Just the other side? Then back again straightaway?'

'No,' Pluck said patiently. 'Not straightaway. Back again tomorrow.'

'Listen...' the wolf said. 'If you think of somewhere really far away, anywhere, just tell me, then we'll go there. It'll be fun. OK?'

The wolf rowed on through the fog.

'Ten long years!' he shouted again. 'You're the first person in ten long years!'

'I think it's because of that sign,' Pluck said. 'Your sign says TELL ME WHERE-WOLF. And now people think you're a werewolf. And a werewolf is a lot worse than an ordinary wolf.'

'Really?' the wolf said. 'Is that it? I thought it was because of the cabbage and the goat.'

'What? What about a cabbage and a goat?'

'I once ate a cabbage,' the wolf said.

'A cabbage?' Pluk said. 'But wolves don't eat cabbages.'

'No, that's true. But this cabbage was inside a goat. It was packaged in a goat.'

'Ah, you ate a goat?'

The wolf nodded. 'A very long time ago...' he said softly and Pluck could tell from his eyes that he was very ashamed of himself.

'Let's just forget about it...' Pluck said. 'After all, I've eaten chickens sometimes. Roasted, of course.'

'This is it,' the wolf said. He had moored on the bank. They had crossed the river.

'Shall we just go back and forth a couple of times quickly?' the wolf asked longingly.

'I'll be back tomorrow,' Pluck said. 'I promise. But now I have to keep going. Do you know which road leads to the hermite?'

The wolf shook his head. 'There's only one road,' he said. 'It goes to Hasselworth.'

'That's where I have to go,' Pluck cried. 'He lives in Hasselworth.'

He drove his truck off the boat and asked, 'What do I owe you?'

'Nothing,' the wolf said. 'Nothing at all. I'm so grateful you took my ferry. So grateful! And I'll stay here to wait for you. See you tomorrow!'

'See you tomorrow,' Pluck said.

And he drove off.

Not Much Time

Pluck had finally made it to the other side of the river. And the fog was all gone. But... it was already evening.

After he had driven his tow truck for half an hour it was as dark as dark can be...

'I have to get to Hasselworth,' Pluck said to himself. 'But how am I going to find it? I can't see where I am at all.'

The road he was driving on was tiny and very quiet, with trees on both sides. His headlights weren't very bright and he couldn't see if there were any houses or farms anywhere. He couldn't see anything except the trees and the roadside and he kept driving until the road forked.

And I can't see any signposts... no signs at all... Pluck thought. *Should I turn right? Or should I go left?* He pulled over and got the shell out of his pocket.

'Should I turn right or left?' he asked.

The Tootenlisp didn't answer. It had turned into a dead empty shell and wasn't even making a rustling noise anymore. Was it still cross at him? Pluck had been a bit gruff with the Tootenlisp earlier that day. He hadn't believed it when it gave him directions. You probably had to be very careful with Tootenlisps and always believe them, otherwise they'd get cross and never give you directions again. *I'll ask it straight out,* Pluck thought.

He raised the shell up to his mouth and whispered, 'Are you still cross with me, Tootenlisp? Can't you give me directions just one last time? I'm sorry I was mean to you. And for not believing you.'

The shell didn't make any sound at all and Pluck sighed. But he didn't give up, he kept talking, 'It's already Tuesday night, Tootenlisp. And on Thursday the bulldozers are going to start work in Dovey Gardens. That's the day after tomorrow! And if we don't get help soon they'll destroy everything, all of Dovey Gardens with everything in it, all the animals and plants. And the only one who can help us is the hermite and he lives somewhere near here. In Hasselworth. But where is Hasselworth? Say something, Tootenlisp... please!' No answer. Pluck put the shell back in his pocket. He took the blanket he'd brought with him and draped it over his shoulders. *I'll get some sleep,* he thought sadly. *There's no sense in searching for a hermite in total darkness.*

He ate his last sandwich. Jam. Above him, the wind rustled through the tree tops. And Pluck felt like the branches were murmuring, 'Too late... you'll be too late... too late...'

And with all that rustling and murmuring, Pluck fell asleep, exhausted, even before he'd finished his sandwich.

In the Pill Building it was night time too and everyone was asleep. And the whole park was asleep. And in Dovey Gardens all the animals were asleep, except for an old owl who was keeping watch and cried 'Ooh' every now and then. The only one who couldn't sleep was

Mr Penn from the bookshop. He was lying in bed in a small room at the back of his shop in his new pyjamas. And he couldn't sleep because he was worried about Pluck.

I should never have sent the boy off by himself, he thought. *After all, he's just a little boy with a*

little tow truck. And it was misty all day. It was foggy. What if he drove into the river by mistake. The River Haze! What if he got lost?

Mr Penn grew more and more anxious and at first light he got up and went out onto the pavement in his beautiful pyjamas.

It was extremely early and there was no one out on the street, but fortunately Dolly flew up after a while.

'Guess, what I just saw!' she called out without saying good morning. She was very agitated, that was obvious.

'Tell me,' Mr Penn said.

'A hundred million paving stones!' Dolly cried. 'Last night trucks and trucks full of paving stones arrived. They're piled up in the park next to the path to Dovey Gardens!'

'You don't think they're going to start today, do you?' Mr Penn asked fearfully.

'I don't know,' Dolly said.

'Keep a close eye on them,' Mr Penn said. 'And if the bulldozers start this morning, come and tell me right away. Then we'll try to move as many animals to safety as possible. Oh, oh, oh... if only I hadn't sent Pluck away. He could have helped with his tow truck. Maybe he got lost in the fog... or drove into the river... I'm so scared he hasn't found the hermite.'

'Shall I go and look for Pluck?' Dolly asked. 'I can fly fast when I need to. And I know where the River Haze is.'

Mr Penn hesitated for a moment, then said, 'That's very nice of you, Dolly, but we need you here. You have to keep an eye on Dovey Gardens. To make sure nothing happens.'

'OK,' Dolly said. She was actually quite relieved, because she didn't know the way that well, not all the way to the River Haze. And then they heard a shrill cry overhead. 'Ahoy! Ahoy!'

'It's Carl,' said Mr Penn happily.

Yes, it was Carl with the wooden leg.

'Can you go and look for Pluck?' Mr Penn shouted. 'He's on the other side of the River Haze. In Hasselworth! Looking for the hermite!'

'No worries!' Carl shouted. 'I'm on my way! Ahoy!'

'Wait!' Mr Penn cried. 'Not so fast. Did you hear *exactly* what I said?'

'Yep!' Carl called.

'Repeat it back to me then!'

'I have to go to the other side of the River Haze!' Carl called.

'Correct. And?'

'Look for the Hasselmite!'

'No!' Mr Penn stamped his foot on the ground and said, 'Come and sit down quietly. We can't talk while you're flying around.'

After Carl had sat on a post, Mr Penn told him slowly and clearly what had happened. And where to look for Pluck.

'I don't know where exactly Hasselworth is either,' he said. 'Or where exactly the hermite lives, but with your sharp eyes you should be able to find Pluck's tow truck. Then help him

any way you can. And tell him he has to be back home tonight. Because early tomorrow morning at the latest, they'll start work with the bulldozers... and don't waste any time, Carl, and don't forget...'

'Yeah, yeah, can I go now?' Carl cried impatiently. 'If you keep talking all day, I won't make it.'

'Go then,' said Mr Penn. 'Go.'

And Carl went. With three big flaps of his wings he was out of sight.

Heading south. To the River Haze.

The Hasselwood

The sun was shining on Pluck's blanket when he woke up. He looked around with surprise and didn't know where he was. Was he sleeping outside? In his tow truck? And then he remembered.

Quickly he turned off his headlights, which he'd left on. He had gone to sleep the night before because he didn't know which way to go. And now he couldn't waste a minute because it was already Wednesday. He only had this one day to find the hermite. Tomorrow the bulldozers would arrive to destroy Dovey Gardens. Oh, yeah, he had to choose between the road going right and the road going left. He took a chance and turned left. And then he heard it very clearly in his pocket, '*Toooo-toooo...*' The Tootenlisp! He stopped, pulled the shell out of his pocket and said, 'Hello!' And there it was, the small whispering voice in his ear, 'Thith ith the wrong way.'

'Should I take the right then?' Pluck asked. 'Does that lead to Hasselworth?'

'Hathelworth ith right,' said the Tootenlisp.

'Thanks! Tell me, why wouldn't you talk to me last night? Were you still cross with me?'

At first there wasn't any answer. Then, after a long time, the shell said, 'Maybe I wath athleep.'

'Oh,' said Pluck. He laid the Tootenlisp down next to him and started driving. It was a lonely stretch of countryside with endless boring fields, hardly any trees and just the odd farmhouse in the distance now and then.

Last night he'd eaten half of his last sandwich. Now he ate the rest. He was hungry and it seemed as if the road would never end. Finally he saw a few trees on a small hill on the left of the road.

'*Tooo-tooo...*' said the Tootenlisp. 'Thtop!'

'Is this Hasselworth?' Pluck asked.

'Yeth. And thith ith the Hathelwood. Thothe are hathel treeth.'

'Is this where the hermite lives?'

'Thith ith it,' said the shell.

Pluck got out. He walked around the three big trees. They were hassel trees. That was what the Tootenlisp had said. They were tall with thick trunks and enormous crowns. He climbed up onto a hill and looked around. There wasn't a house anywhere.

'There's no house,' he said to the shell.

'There ith a houthe.'

'Where?'

'You're thtanding on it.'

Pluck looked down. He couldn't see anything except the ground he was standing on, some grass and some bushes. There wasn't any house.

He almost got angry. He almost shouted, 'Look for yourthelf, you thilly thea thell!'

But fortunately he stopped himself just in time. Making the Tootenlisp cross was not a good idea.

Pluck sighed and had a closer look between the bushes. And then he found an aerial. A TV aerial stuck in the top of the hill.

The house is inside the hill, Pluck thought. He walked down the slope looking for a door,

On holiday until
13th November

then walked once around the hill without finding anything. Then he peeked behind an overhanging bush. And there was a door. A real door. The hill was a house. He knocked on the door. Nothing happened. He pushed on the door and tried the handle, but it was locked. And only then did he see the piece of paper. Written on it in big letters, it said: *On holiday until 13th November.*

This was too much for Pluck. He sat down on the ground next to the two empty milk bottles and started sobbing. It had all been for nothing. The whole, long, difficult trip!

All for nothing. And he felt so alone. And he was so hungry. He held the Tootenlisp up to his mouth and said, 'Hey, Tootenlisp. He's not home.'

The Tootenlisp rustled softly, but didn't say anything in reply.

Pluck didn't cry for long. He had sobbed three times. And shed a single tear. Now he got up and went back to his truck. He had to hurry back home to the Pill Building. They needed him there. He could use his tow truck to move as many animals to safety as possible.

He'd only driven about twenty yards when

he heard a voice above him. 'Ahoy!' It was Carl with the wooden leg! Pluck stopped immediately. At last, someone to talk to.

Carl landed on his truck and said, 'You were so hard to find! I crossed the river hours ago. But you were nowhere in sight. I flew high and low searching for you... and finally I saw something red between all that green. A red dot, your truck. Tell me, have you seen the hermite? Did you find his house?'

'Yes, but he's not home,' Pluck said. 'He's on holiday until November.'

'Oh, bad luck,' said the seagull.

'He lives in that hill,' Pluck said. 'But that's no help. I'm going home. How are things there? They haven't started on Dovey Gardens yet have they?'

'No,' Carl said, 'it's still quiet. Mr Penn sent me to look for you, he was worried. I'll fly back now. I'll tell them you're coming. Bye.'

'Bye,' said Pluck.

Carl flew off, but a moment later he was back again.

'Hey!' he screeched. 'Did the hermite leave his kids behind? I just flew over those trees,' Carl said, 'and I saw bubbles.'

'Bubbles?'

'Yes, someone's blowing bubbles. Beautiful, coloured bubbles floating up above that middle tree.'

Pluck turned his truck around and drove back. 'Fly over that tree, Carl,' he said. 'And yell as loud as you can. I'll stand under it and yell.'

'Ahoy!' Carl called. And screeching loudly he fluttered around just over the top of the middle tree, while Pluck stood below it shouting, 'Hello, is anyone there? Her-mite!?'

But Carl flew down to the ground. 'There's no point,' he said. 'He's not in the tree.'

'How do you know?' Pluck asked.

'An arm came up out of the tree,' Carl said.

I am not here

'With a sign. And the sign said: *I am not here*.'

'So who was holding the sign?' Pluck asked.

'I don't know,' Carl said. 'Someone with an arm.'

'And who's the "I" who's not here?'

'I don't know,' Carl said.

Just then something fell down out of the tree. It landed right next to Pluck. It was a slipper.

And a little later something else fell out of the tree, with a bang. A bowl of soapsuds. The soapsuds splashed out and the bowl lay upside-down on the ground.

'Hello, hermite!' Pluck called. 'I can see you! Come down out of the tree!'

And then slowly, very slowly, someone lowered themselves down out of the tree. Upside-down, headfirst. The way cats sometimes climb down out of trees. A head with a beard. And then the rest of the hermite.

He looked terribly sad and mumbled, 'I'll just make some new suds.'

'Mr Hermite, sir,' Pluck said. 'A friend of yours sent me, Mr Penn. May I come in for a moment?'

The hermite hesitated.

'Mr Penn sent you?' he said. 'Come in then.'

A Very Weird Man

Pluck was at the hermite's. The house was inside the hill. It was just a round room with a tiny kitchen. And no windows anywhere.

There was only one chair and Pluck was sitting on it. He had a big bowl of porridge in front of him and he was so hungry he was shovelling it in.

The hermite was lying on the bed. 'Well, well,' he said, 'Mr Penn sent you.'

'Yes,' said Pluck with his mouth full. He had just told him the whole story. About Dovey Gardens being cut down and all the frightened and desperate animals huddling together. About the mouse family with the bald baby mice and how sad it was. And he had also told him that he was in a terrible rush.

The hermite nodded. He was a friendly man, but sometimes he didn't seem to be listening at all. As if he was thinking about something completely different.

'Mr Penn said you could help us,' Pluck said.

He'd finished the porridge and wiped his mouth off with the back of his hand. Then he wiped his hand on his trousers.

'I'll have to think about it first,' the hermite said. He stretched out on the bed and closed his eyes.

'Why does it say *On holiday until 13th November* on the door?' Pluck asked.

'I always leave that up,' the hermite said. 'I don't like visitors.'

'But what if visitors come on the thirteenth of November?' Pluck asked inquisitively.

'I change the note the day before,' the hermite said. 'Then it says *On holiday until 13th March.*'

'Oh,' said Pluck. 'And just before the thirteenth of March...'

'That's right,' the hermite said. 'Then I change it back again. That way I never get any visitors.'

'I always thought it was "hermit",' Pluck said. 'With IT on the end.'

'A hermit is a completely different thing to a hermite,' the hermite said.

'What's the difference?'

'I'll have to think about that,' the hermite said. He closed his eyes again. He looked like he was asleep.

Pluck was getting impatient. He was in a hurry. He wanted to leave. And now this weird man was lying here thinking... about something else that had nothing to do with it.

'Will you please think about helping instead?' he asked

'Helping? Helping with what?'

Pluck sighed. Did he have to tell the whole story over again?

'With Dovey Gardens,' he said.

'Oh, yes, that's right...' the hermite said.

'Well?' Pluck asked. 'Can you help us?'

'It's a real shame you've come at the wrong time,' the hermite said. 'There aren't any hasselberries at the moment. You saw it yourself outside. Not a single hasselberry on any of the hassel trees. It's much too early. That's all there is to it.'

He closed his eyes again and fell silent.

'Oh,' Pluck said. 'And, um... are hassel-berries the only way? Of helping, I mean?'

'Of course,' the hermite said. 'That goes without saying. Come back in about eight weeks. There'll be loads of them then.'

'What good is that!' Pluck cried. 'That's too late. You have to help me today. Can't you come up with something else?'

'I'll try,' the hermite said, stretching out on the bed again.

It took a very, very long time. Pluck looked around and saw that the clock already said twelve o'clock. The day was half over. He still had to start the long trip home. He still had to cross the river on the ferry...

Then he heard quiet snoring. The hermite really *had* fallen asleep.

136

Pluck coughed loudly. The hermite shot up.

'Is there a fire?' he cried in fright.

'No,' Pluck said. 'I want to know if you've thought about it.'

'Thought about it? What am I supposed to think about?'

Pluck was getting desperate. And now he was very angry. 'Listen,' he raged. 'I have to go. I don't have any more time. You're not even trying to help!'

He got up and walked to the door.

'Thanks for the porridge,' he added.

And he went outside to his truck, where Carl was sitting waiting.

'Did it work?' Carl asked.

'No,' Pluck said angrily. 'He's a very weird man. He keeps falling asleep. And he can't think of anything. I'm leaving, otherwise I won't get back home today.'

But when Pluck started to drive off, Carl cried, 'Wait! He's got something.'

Pluck stopped. The hermite had come out of the house with a gigantic flowerpot. He carried it over to the tow truck.

'Here,' he told Pluck. 'Just try it.'

'What am I supposed to do with that?' Pluck asked. There was a very small plant in the pot. With drooping leaves.

'Plant it...' the hermite said. 'Just stick it in the ground.'

'Where?' Pluck asked.

'Where they pass by, of course,' said the hermite.

'Where who passes by?'

The hermite closed his eyes, thought for a moment and said, 'Oh, that's right, now I remember... I have to make some new suds! So I can blow bubbles.' And he hurried into the house.

'A dead plant!' Carl cried. 'How will that help!'

'I told you he's weird,' Pluck said.

He put the flowerpot on his truck and said, 'You fly ahead, back to the Pill Building. Tell Mr Penn I'm coming.'

'Do you know the way back?' Carl asked. 'You should take the big ferry, that's the shortest route. From here you just drive straight.'

'OK,' Pluck said. But then he suddenly thought of the wolf. The tell me where-wolf with his little boat. He'd promised to cross back over the river with the wolf.

For a moment he wavered... it was already so late... and he was in such a hurry.

'Listen, Carl,' he said. 'Could you fly past the wolf on the way? Tell him I won't come today. Tell him I'll cross the river with him again some other time.'

'Wolf?' Carl asked. 'What wolf?'

'Oh, of course... you don't know about that yet,' Pluck said. 'There's another ferry over the river... a little one. And the ferryman is a wolf, but a very friendly wolf, and he's waiting for me, you see.'

'Oh, yeah,' Carl said. 'I saw him! I couldn't tell he was a wolf. I was too high up for that. But I saw the boat. It was all decorated!'

'Decorated?'

'Yes, with flowers... I think,' Carl said.

Pluck sighed. 'Don't say anything then,' he said. 'If the wolf's decorated his boat for me... Well, I can't let him down. I'll cross the river on his little ferryboat.'

'Ahoy!' Carl cried, flying off. Heading north to the Pill Building.

Wednesday

When Pluck reached the River Haze it was already fairly late in the afternoon. Wednesday afternoon... He had to be back home that evening... because early tomorrow morning they'd start! That was when the bulldozers were going to flatten Dovey Gardens.

Pluck saw it from a distance: the wolf's boat looked amazing. It was covered with flowers! Garlands of daisies and dandelions.

And on the bank the wolf started waving and called out from a distance, 'Hooray, you've come after all... Hooray! I've been waiting all day!'

Pluck was glad he hadn't taken the big ferry. The wolf would have been heartbroken if he hadn't come.

He parked his tow truck on the ferry and the wolf started rowing.

'I've got a nice surprise for you,' he said.

'Really?' Pluck said. 'What?'

'I'm going to row you all the way to the waterfall,' the wolf said. 'Up in the mountains.'

'No!' Pluck cried out in fright. 'No. Please don't.'

The wolf lowered his oars in disappointment and asked, 'Why not? It's beautiful!'

'Listen, tell me where-wolf,' Pluck said. 'I don't have time! I'm in a big hurry. They're waiting for me back home. I have to go straight across the river. I have to get the other side as fast as possible. Please, keep rowing!'

The wolf didn't do it. He sulked. He left the oars dangling and didn't do a thing.

'You know what?' Pluck said. 'I'll come back sometime! I promise, I'll come back and when I do you can take me wherever you like. But not now! Now you have to row!' But the wolf just sat there with an angry face.

'And you know what else?' Pluck said. 'I'll tell everyone you're the best ferryman there is. With the best ferry. I'll tell them and then loads of people will go on your boat.'

The wolf started to look a little more cheerful. 'Really?' he asked. 'Promise?'

'I promise,' Pluck said. 'But first you have to row.'

And now the colourful, flowery boat shot through the water. It went straight to the other side and they were there in just a few minutes.

'Bye!' Pluck called, when he was back on dry land with his truck. 'You can count on me! I'll see you next time.'

The wolf stood there waving goodbye for a very long time. He was still waving long after Pluck had disappeared out of sight.

Mr Penn stood outside on the pavement waiting with Dolly on his shoulder. He looked at his watch. 'Five o'clock...' he moaned. 'Five o'clock on Wednesday afternoon! And still no sign of Pluck. And no Carl either... Oh, Dolly, I'm so worried...'

'Stand still for a moment...' Dolly said. 'I think that's Carl there in the distance.'

'Ahoy!' they heard faintly, then louder and louder. 'Ahoy!'

After Carl had landed, the first thing Mr Penn asked was, 'Where's Pluck? Have you found him?'

'Pluck's on his way,' Carl said. 'He's fine.'

'Thank goodness,' Mr Penn sighed. 'That's the main thing. Did he find the hermite?'

'Yes,' Carl said. 'But it didn't help a bit.'

'It didn't help?'

'The hermite couldn't think of anything,' Carl said. 'Just a dead plant.'

'A dead plant?'

'A scrawny little dead plant. That's what he gave Pluck.'

'What good's a plant going to do us?' Dolly exclaimed. 'I knew it wouldn't help. And tomorrow the bulldozers are coming. We have to try to rescue the animals. They have to move out of Dovey Gardens before dark! To somewhere else in the park where it's safe.'

'Let's wait a little longer...' Mr Penn said, 'for Pluck –'

'Too late!' Dolly screeched. 'It'll be dark before he gets here. Everyone in Dovey Gardens will be asleep.'

'I'd still rather wait for Pluck,' Mr Penn said. 'The hermite's given him a plant... Did he say what we had to do with it?'

'He didn't say anything!' Carl cried. 'He's a very weird man. He just handed over a big flowerpot with a dead plant in it. That's all.'

'If you're not coming, I'll go by myself!' Dolly cried. 'I'm going to warn the animals. I'll tell them to flee before it gets too dark.'

Mr Penn called out weakly, 'Just wait... don't be so hasty...' But Dolly was gone.

'Is there anything else I can do for you?' Carl asked. 'If not, I'll go catch a fish in the harbour. I didn't stop to eat on the way, so...'

'Go ahead,' Mr Penn said. 'We can't do anything right now anyway. And thanks for your help.'

Carl flew off, leaving Mr Penn behind on the pavement. Every now and then, when a customer arrived, he would pop into his shop to serve them. But otherwise he stayed outside. Into the evening. When it grew darker and darker... until finally the tow truck's little headlights came round the corner.

'At last...' Mr Penn said. 'I've been so worried. Quick, tell me if the hermite can help us.'

'No,' Pluck said. 'At least... this is all he gave me.'

He dragged the heavy flowerpot out of the truck.

'And what are we supposed to do with it?' Mr Penn asked.

'Plant it.'

'Where?'

'I don't know.'

'Didn't the hermite say anything at all? Like where to plant it?'

Pluck thought for a moment, then said, 'Where they pass by, that's what he said.'

'Where they pass by? Who?'

'That's what I asked,' Pluck said. 'But he didn't answer.'

'Where they pass by...' Mr Penn mumbled. 'I think I almost understand... He means where the workers will pass by early tomorrow morning on their way to Dovey Gardens. We'll plant it right next to the path to Dovey Gardens. In the park. Come on... we'll do it right away. I'll just grab a watering can with some water.'

They put the flower pot back on the truck and drove to the park.

It was completely dark by the time Pluck and Mr Penn planted the scrawny little plant in the park in the light of Pluck's headlights. They sprinkled water over it with the watering can, but Mr Penn said despondently, 'That thing is as dead as a doornail. It's had it.'

Just when they were about to drive back, Dolly came out of Dovey Gardens. Walking, because she was exhausted and too sleepy to fly.

'Hello,' she said. 'They all refuse.'

'Who?' Pluck asked. 'What?'

'They refuse to leave,' Dolly said. 'They won't leave Dovey Gardens. They all say the same thing. They'd rather die than move. What do you say to that?'

'Let's get some sleep,' Mr Penn said. 'We've done what we can. We'll come back tomorrow morning. All three of us. We'll meet here in this spot. Then we'll take it from there.'

The Hasselberries

It was Thursday morning, 'danger day'! In the park, next to the bags of cement and the stacks of paving stones, a big bulldozer was waiting.

Pluck and Mr Penn were with Dolly, standing over the small plant they had planted the night before.

'Dead as a dodo!' Dolly cried.

'Yes, it's died,' Mr Penn sighed. 'I still don't know why the hermite gave us a plant... I was hoping it was a magic plant... but even a magic plant's no use to us dead.'

'Now we have to hurry and move all of the animals in Dovey Gardens to safety,' Pluck said. 'We've got half an hour. At eight o'clock the workers arrive. Then the bulldozer will flatten everything... Come on!'

They got into the tow truck and drove down the narrow path to Dovey Gardens. There, at the frog pool, the terrified animals were gathered together. Birds and mice and hedgehogs. Moles and rabbits. Four fat rats and a squirrel. Plus all the littlies: things like caterpillars and crickets and beetles, but they were off to one side in the tall grass.

'There's Pluck!' they cried. 'Pluck will protect us! He'll chase the angry men away with his mighty tow truck!'

Pluck shook his head sadly and said, 'No, I can't chase them away. But I can help you escape. I'll put you in my truck, everyone except the birds. They can fly.

'Hey!' a little bird shouted. 'What about my nest? I've got a nest, you know!'

'I can take the nests with me,' Pluck said.

'And us?' cried the father mouse. 'What about me and my family? My poor, bald little babies?'

'Everyone's coming,' Pluck said. 'I'll drive back and forth a few times. But we need to hurry because they're about to start! Come on.'

Now the squirrel stepped forward and said, 'Do you remember me?'

'It's Dizzy!' Mr Penn exclaimed. 'The squirrel who was afraid of heights.'

'That's right,' Dizzy said. 'I live here. And I've got a nest with little squirrels in it. And I don't want to leave. None of us want to leave.'

'That's right...' the other animals shouted, 'we're staying here. No matter what. We're not going. We'd rather be run over!'

'You're mad!' Dolly cried. 'Think of your children. Everything here is going to be destroyed... there won't be any trees left...'

'I'll be very careful with your nests,' Pluck said.

But no matter how much they begged or threatened, it didn't help. What a stubborn crowd. And then they heard the rumbling of a heavy truck. 'That's them!' Pluck cried. 'They're about to start! Who wants to be rescued?'

But the animals shot off in all directions. In the blink of an eye they were back in their holes and nests, trembling and waiting for the disaster to strike.

'Come on,' Mr Penn said, taking Pluck by

the arm and dragging him back down the path towards the park.

There was the big truck. Four or five men had climbed out and were looking around.

'Quick... over here...' Mr Penn whispered.

Without making a sound, they hid behind a bush... Looking through the leaves, they had a perfect view of what was happening.

One of the men had climbed up onto the biggest bulldozer. The others were about to follow the path to Dovey Gardens, when suddenly they stopped.

'What are they doing now?' Mr Penn whispered.

'They're picking something from a bush...' Pluck whispered back, 'and eating it.'

Mr Penn peered through the leaves. Then he said, 'That bush! That wasn't there before... Pluck! It's our little plant!'

He was right. Their scrawny little plant had

turned into a bush when the sun shone on it. A bush full of purple berries.

Now the bulldozer came driving towards them with a terrible roar. It was only a few seconds away... it was about to crush them... but then it stopped. The man climbed down. The others gave him a handful of berries.

Pluck and Mr Penn held their breath and waited.

Then something completely unexpected happened: the men started running around. They skipped between the stacks of paving stones and chased each other and yelled and screamed like little boys.

A very surprised Mr Penn said, 'I think they're going to play hide and seek.'

And he was right. They started to play hide and seek. A car drove up, a beautiful fancy car. And out stepped the Park Master. With his eyebrows raised, he stared at one of the workers, who was standing next to a tree counting. 'One, two, three... hundred! Here I come ready or not!'

'Ready or not?' the Park Master raged. 'I'll give you ready or not! Aren't you ashamed of yourselves? Playing hide and seek in work hours. Grown-up men. Bah!'

Then the hasselberry bush caught his eye. Without thinking, he picked a couple of berries and popped them in his mouth.

'Well, what about it? You going to start work?' he yelled. 'Or do I have to –' He fell silent. And the anger disappeared from his face. He grinned.

'Wait a minute. I'm playing too!' he shouted. Whooping and screaming he joined the others.

'It's because of the berries...' Mr Penn said, 'the hasselberries. They're playberries. As soon as you eat them, you want to play instead of work.'

Now the Park Master was coming towards

them. He looked behind the bush, found them there and screamed with delight. 'You're it!' he shouted at Mr Penn, tapping him on the shoulder. Then he ran off.

'Me?' Mr Penn said. 'Am I supposed to play hide and seek too?'

'Stay here. I'll go,' Pluck said, running off to join in with all the cheerful men in the park. Their game got very wild. Meanwhile Dolly was talking to Mr Penn.

'It worked!' she said. 'Shall I go and tell the animals in Dovey Gardens they're saved? That it's all safe? The men aren't working. Now they'll keep playing for the rest of their lives. Shall I go and tell them?'

'I don't think it's permanent,' Mr Penn said anxiously. 'It might wear off in an hour or two... the effect is probably temporary.'

'Come, now,' said Dolly. 'Eat some berries!'

'I just might,' said Mr Penn. 'They look delicious.'

The bush was still almost full of big purple berries. It seemed to keep growing new ones. Mr Penn ate a few.

In the park the men had now made a beautiful slide. And everyone slid down it.

The Park Master and the workmen and Pluck... 'Yippy-eye-ay!' shouted Mr Penn. And he raced over to have a go on the slide.

'So,' Dolly said. And she went to Dovey Gardens to tell the animals that the danger had passed. And that they were safe. 'For now...' she added, but the animals didn't hear that bit. They were too busy celebrating.

Grown-ups Playing

The bush in the park grew and grew and kept sprouting new berries. Nobody could walk past without tasting one. And everybody who tasted one started to play. Because the hasselberry was a playberry.

People who went to the park could hardly believe their eyes. Everywhere, grown-ups were playing games. Five plump ladies were dancing in a circle and singing nursery rhymes. A very old gentleman was making sandcastles on the pile of sand, together with an old lady. The doctor and the minister were playing leap-frog, the butcher and the baker were on a see-saw and you could hear laughing and whooping everywhere.

Nobody even thought about working. The men with the bulldozer had forgotten all about flattening Dovey Gardens.

When they got tired of tag and hide and seek... they started to play with the cement mixer. They made all kinds of fantastic shapes from paving stones and sand and tools and

then poured concrete over them. The result was some very strange-looking statues.

Of course, the children joined in too. You could see them running around all over the place. They pushed the wheelbarrows and Pluck played blind man's buff with the Park Master. The only one who didn't join in was Mrs Brightner.

She had come to the park to see what was happening. And now she was looking on furiously. She grabbed the Park Master by the sleeve and snarled, 'What is all this mess?

You should be working on Dovey Gardens! And now you're playing like a little child. Shame on you. That's no way for a Park Master to behave!'

'Now, now, don't nag!' the Park Master exclaimed, running off. But Pluck came up to Mrs Brightner with a handful of juicy berries.

'Try some...' he said, 'they're delicious.'

Mrs Brightner peered at the purple fruit and said, 'They haven't been washed, have they? No, thanks, much too dirty.'

Then she went up to a workman who was building a crazy concrete tower. 'If you don't start work immediately,' she shouted, 'I shall telephone the mayor.'

'You don't need to phone him,' the man laughed. 'He's right there. Just behind you.'

Mrs Brightner turned around and there was the mayor. He had heard that something special was happening, put on his best suit and come to the park.

'Thank goodness you're here!' cried Mrs Brightner. 'The whole town's gone mad. Just look what they're doing!'

'Yes...' the mayor said with a surprised expression, looking around at all the playing and whooping people.

'You have to do something!' said Mrs Brightner. 'Send in the police immediately.'

'The police?' the mayor said, pointing. 'They're already here.'

A little bit further along two policemen were playing hopscotch. They'd drawn numbers on paving stones and were squealing with delight.

'Outrageous!' Mrs Brightner cried. 'And have you seen all those enormous crazy things they're making with the concrete?'

The mayor held his head a little to one side and looked carefully at the fanciful shapes and statues.

'I like them...' he said. 'They're quite artistic!'

'Artistic!' Mrs Brightner screamed. 'It's rubbish! A waste of valuable resources!'

But the mayor simply pushed her out of the way to get a better look.

'Real works of art...' he whispered, 'just what I've always wanted. I always wanted big beautiful sculptures in our park. But we never had enough money. And now we've got them after all... just like that. I'm completely bowled over!'

'But...' Mrs Brightner moaned. 'What about Dovey Gardens? That dirty messy

patch of forest back there! The plan was to turn it into a nice paved square. And now they've used up all the paving stones!'

The mayor looked around. It was true. They had used all the paving stones playing and building sculptures.

He shrugged. 'Yes,' he said. 'We certainly can't afford to buy new paving stones.'

'You mean you're going to leave Dovey Gardens the way it is?' Mrs Brightner shouted angrily.

'I never really liked the idea of cutting down all those trees,' the mayor said. 'I'm actually glad to keep a bit of real forest. For the children to play in. And for birds to nest in.'

'And you're going to leave these ugly shapes and statues here? In our park?' Mrs Brightner asked.

'Yes,' the mayor said, beaming with pleasure. 'They're going to stay here permanently.' And he skipped off... That was strange because he hadn't eaten any berries. But it does happen... Some people don't need hasselberries to skip and play, it just comes naturally.

Almost choking with fury, Mrs Brightner went home.

There was someone who had overhead the conversation. It was Dolly the pigeon. She flew over to Pluck to tell him all about it.

'It is permanent!' she said. 'They're not going to clear Dovey Gardens after all... the animals are saved. Go tell them, Pluck.'

When Pluck arrived in Dovey Gardens, all the animals had crept off. It was very quiet at the frog pool. There was no croaking and no birds were cheeping. It was only after Pluck had whistled softly, that a small frightened animal appeared.

It was the father mouse. He was very nervous and his whiskers were trembling.

'Are the angry men coming after all?' he asked. 'Are they coming to destroy our forest?'

'No,' Pluck said. 'No, don't be scared.'

'But we heard such a terrible racket...' the mouse said. 'Droning and roaring... What was that?'

'That's the cement mixer,' Pluck said. 'But they're not doing anything with it. They're just playing. And they're not coming here.'

'Can I tell my wife and babies they can relax and go to sleep?' the mouse asked. 'They haven't slept all week, you know.'

'Go and tell them,' Pluck said. 'And tell everyone else who lives here too. The danger has passed. Forever!'

'Thank you,' said the father mouse.

And Pluck ran back to the park to play some more.

Everything Goes Wrong!

Pluck whistled as he walked along the walkway on the fourteenth floor. He was on his way to the lift. He wanted to go down to the street, where all the grown-ups were playing.

A very old woman was standing outside the door of one of the flats. She had a big bandage on her leg and she was looking in the rubbish bin. Pluck was amazed to see her fish a piece of stale bread out of the bin... and eat it!

'Hello,' he said. He knew her very well, it was old Aunty Nettie.

'Ah! Pluck!' she called. 'I'm glad to see you! Everyone's gone out to play! There's no one left in the Pill Building.'

'Have you hurt your leg?' Pluck asked.

'That's just it,' said Aunty Nettie. 'Yesterday I fell over skipping. And I hurt my leg. And now I tried to call the doctor, but he's out playing on the street! Oh, Pluck... it's all too horrible.'

Poor Aunty Nettie burst into tears and Pluck felt very sorry for her.

'And I'm so hungry...' she sobbed. 'That's why I was looking for bread in the rubbish bin... because the baker doesn't deliver anymore. He's off playing somewhere.'

'Just be patient,' Pluck said. 'I'll go and get the doctor. And I'll buy some bread.'

'And milk too,' said Aunty Nettie. 'Because the milkman's running around the neighbourhood playing tag.'

'I'll take care of it,' Pluck said and he went to go, but Aunty Nettie stopped him, saying, 'There's something else... there's a terrible leak too.'

'Where?' Pluck asked. He looked up and in the same instant an enormous gush of water splashed down on his face.

'The pipes have burst,' Aunty Nettie said. 'It's leaking everywhere. Look!'

Pluck saw water running down the walls and dripping from the balconies.

'The plumber needs to come straight-away,' he said.

'I tried to call him,' Aunty Nettie said. 'But no-one answered. He's probably playing marbles.'

Pluck went downstairs in the lift. When he was outside, he stopped on the pavement to look around. It was as if the fun fair had come to town. The whole neighbourhood was one big playground. Grown-ups and kids... all in a big whirl, everyone screaming and shoving, playing games everywhere. Nobody going to work and not one child at school anymore, because the teachers were all playing on the street. A fat lady was bouncing a ball against a wall and Pluck asked her if she'd seen the doctor anywhere.

'The doctor's up in that tree,' she said. 'With the lawyer's wife.'

Pluck peered upwards. Very high up between the leaves, he could see a pair of legs dangling down. 'Doctor!' he called.

Now the doctor's face appeared, peeking down through the leaves.

'Could you come for a moment?' Pluck called. 'To look at Aunty Nettie's leg!'

'No!' the doctor called back. 'I'm having too much fun playing!' And his face disappeared again.

Pluck decided to buy some bread. But now he saw that all the shops were closed. Every one, including Mr Penn's bookshop. And the baker was playing with the milkman. They were playing skittles with empty milk bottles and a plastic ball and they ignored Pluck when he asked if there was anywhere he could get some bread and milk. And now he saw the plumber too. He was playing cowboys and Indians with the minister.

'Excuse me!' Pluck called. 'Could you come for a moment? There's a leak in the Pill Building!'

'Bang, bang!' the plumber laughed, pretending to shoot him.

Pluck sat down on a step with a heavy heart. No one would listen to him. Everyone was too busy playing. He was just about to go back to the Pill Building when Dolly flew up. She landed on his shoulder and said, 'Pluck! I

just flew over the town and there are such horrible things happening!'

'Like what?' Pluck asked.

'A house burnt down!' Dolly said.
'The people who lived there are on the street!
They lost everything.'

'That's terrible,' Pluck said. 'Wasn't the
fire brigade able to put it out or –' Suddenly
Pluck understood what had happened. 'You
mean the firemen are playing too?'

'Yes,' Dolly said. 'They didn't want to
come. They're playing in the park. I just flew
past... They're making a bonfire with Mr
Penn.'

'I'll go straight there,' Pluck said. And he
ran into the park.

He saw the bonfire the firemen were making. It looked fantastic, that was true. They
kept throwing old boxes and crates onto it,
the flames crackled and, through the smoke,

157

Pluck saw Mr Penn joining in. He was using an axe to cut off dry branches and then throwing them on the fire.

'Mr Penn!' Pluck shouted.

'Not now,' Mr Penn panted. 'I don't have time. I'm playing!'

That made Pluck really angry. If even Mr Penn had stopped listening to him, things really were terrible.

The bush was close by. The hasselberry bush. Full of big fat juicy berries.

'It's all because of those awful berries!' Pluck cried. 'Everyone who eats them starts playing. And the people keep eating them. And it keeps sprouting new berries. And nobody wants to help. They just keep playing.'

In a fury, Pluck snatched the axe out of Mr Penn's hands and started hacking away at the hasselberry bush.

'Hey, what are you doing?' Mr Penn screamed. 'Stop that this instant!' He tried to grab the axe back, but Pluck pushed him away. He chopped and he chopped and the bush was already starting to tilt.

'Help!' Mr Penn cried. 'That boy's chopping our bush down!'

The firemen looked up for a moment. They laughed and said, 'Oh, leave him... he's just playing. We all are.'

Pluck swung the axe one last time and *flop*... the bush was lying on the ground. He dragged it over the path and threw it on the fire.

'What a waste! How terrible!' Mr Penn groaned. 'Pluck, what have you done now?'

But the fire flared up... all kinds of strange colours appeared, blue and green... it was beautiful and people came up on all sides to

watch. Finally everyone was standing around the fire. They'd all stopped playing and they stood there watching until in the end there was nothing left except a messy pile of ash and charcoal and some blackened junk.

The people were silent and a little embarrassed. Nobody was screaming or whooping anymore. And nobody started playing again.

The first one to speak was the doctor. Looking slightly ashamed of himself, he said, 'I've spent the whole day playing and I've let down all my patients. How terrible!'

'I have to go straight to the Pill Building!' cried the plumber. 'I've heard there's a leak!'

'Oh dear...' the baker said, 'no one's delivered any bread all day! I'm such an idiot! Playing games when there's so much work to do.' And he ran off to the bakery.

An hour later everything was back to normal. Aunty Nettie was lying in bed with a cup of tea and a fresh bandage on her leg. The pipes had been fixed and the water had been mopped up. The shops were open again. Only the schools were still closed, but that was because it was already four o'clock in the afternoon. And by then school was over for the day.

Mr Penn stood in his shop and said, 'That was very brave of you, Pluck. Well done! But there's one thing I regret... We should have kept a cutting from that bush. In a flowerpot. Because now all the hasselberries are gone forever and you never know when we might need them.'

Jam

Now that the hasselberry had been cut down, everything was back to normal again. The grown-ups worked every day and had stopped playing. Pluck was a little bored. He wondered whether Aggie was home yet.

Pluck rang Mrs Brightner's doorbell on the nineteenth floor. Timidly, because he was scared of her.

But when she opened the door, she said, 'Hello. Come in, Pluck. You can give me a hand.'

Pluck saw a big, old-fashioned playpen in the hall.

'This has to go in the living room,' Mrs

Brightner said. 'Could you help me for a moment? I have such terrible backache.'

Pluck helped her lug the playpen into the living room and then asked, 'Do you have a baby in the house?'

'A baby? No, this is for Aggie. She's coming home this afternoon.'

'For Aggie?' Pluck cried. 'You're going to put Aggie in a playpen? She's not a baby anymore.'

'No,' Mrs Brightner said. 'But you see, I've just cleaned the whole house. I've painted all the walls white. And if I let Aggie walk around free, everything will get dirty again. That's why she has to go in the playpen. With a rattle. That's cute!'

Pluck was so angry he turned bright red. He forgot that he was scared of Mrs Brightner and shouted, 'I think it's mean!'

Mrs Brightner stared at him with cold eyes. 'It's none of your business,' she said. 'Go away. I don't have time to listen to you. I'm making jam. I've made fifty-four jars of blackberry jam so you can imagine how busy I am!' She pushed Pluck out the front door.

Dazed, he went downstairs to tell Mr Penn.

'In a playpen!' he said at the end. 'She can't do that! A big girl like Aggie in a playpen –'

'Ridiculous!' Mr Penn snorted. 'But tell me... has Aggie been at the seaside all this time?'

'Yes, with the Stamper family. In Egham. And she was as free as a bird there. And now she's going to be shut up in a pen!'

'And that bit about the jam?' Mr Penn asked. 'You said something about blackberry jam.'

'She's made fifty-four jars of blackberry jam. That's what she said.'

'Well, well...' Mr Penn mumbled. 'Where did she get the blackberries?'

'I don't know,' Pluck said. 'She pushed me out the door. Will you please go see her? And tell her it's disgraceful and sick to put Aggie –' Pluck almost choked on his words, that's how angry he was.

'Hmm,' Mr Penn said. 'I'm a little scared of Mrs Brightner. You know what, why don't we go together? You can wait outside on the walkway if you like. But don't leave without me!'

They took the lift up and Mr Penn rang the bell while Pluck stood a little to one side.

When Mrs Brightner opened the door, Mr Penn stepped in bravely and walked straight through to the living room. That was where she'd set up the playpen.

'I hear your daughter is coming home this afternoon,' Mr Penn said.

'That's right,' Mrs Brightner said. 'As you can see, I've got the playpen ready. And I'm terribly busy, so I can't offer you a cup of coffee. I've painted all the walls and my back hurts so much! And I've made jam too!'

Mr Penn peered past her into the kitchen. There were rows and rows of jam jars.

'Blackberry jam?' he asked.

'Fifty-four jars of blackberry jam,' Mrs

Brightner said proudly, showing him into the kitchen. 'I even ran out of jars,' she said. 'I've got a whole saucepan full of jam left over.'

'Where did you buy the blackberries?' Mr Penn asked.

'I didn't buy them,' said Mrs Brightner. 'You could just pick them. In the park. There was a whole bush full of them. I kept going back and forth with a basket.'

'Isn't the jam a little sour?' Mr Penn asked.

'Well, to tell you the truth, I haven't even tasted it yet,' Mrs Brightner said. 'I've been so terribly busy.'

'Blackberry jam is excellent for backache,' said Mr Penn. 'But I'm sure you know that.'

'Is it really?'

'Oh, yes. All the doctors say so. If I were you, I'd try some.'

Mrs Brightner hesitated for a moment. 'All right then, why not...' She dipped the wooden spoon in the saucepan and tasted a big mouthful of jam.

'Mmmm... delicious,' she said. 'Not sour at all. Would you like a taste?'

'No, thank you. I just had breakfast,' Mr Penn said.

'Well,' said Mrs Brightner. 'You can see how busy I am. Thanks for coming to visit. Bye!'

She opened the front door and before he knew it, Mr Penn was back out on the walkway.

Pluck was standing there waiting for him. 'And?' he asked. 'Did you tell her off?'

'No,' said Mr Penn bashfully. 'I didn't get a chance. She bundled me out the door.'

'Let's ring the doorbell again,' Pluck said. 'Then we'll tell her together.'

'I don't dare,' Mr Penn said. 'It's strange, but I'm so scared of her.'

'Me too,' Pluck said. 'But if I'm really angry, I forget that I'm scared.' He pressed the button. No one came to the door.

They rang the doorbell again. Nothing happened. They waited a very long time, then pressed the bell again. And again.

'She hasn't taken ill, has she... suddenly?' Mr Penn said anxiously.

'The door's not locked...' Pluck said. 'We can push it open and go in.'

'It's a bit cheeky,' Mr Penn said. 'But let's do it.'

They went in. They walked through to the living room. There they stopped still. Struck dumb with amazement.

Mrs Brightner was sitting in the playpen. She was playing with the rattle. She was crowing like a baby.

'Are you... quite well?' Mr Penn spluttered.

'Ta-ta!' Mrs Brightner cried happily. And she threw the woollen rabbit out of the pen.

'Goodness me!' Mr Penn whispered. 'She ate too much jam!' He pulled Pluck into the kitchen. The jam jars were still full, but the saucepan was empty.

'Hasselberry jam...' Mr Penn said. 'And hasselberries make you play. You know that. But she's eaten more than a pound of jam in one go! Much too much... and now she's playing in the playpen... like a baby!'

'Da-da!' crowed Mrs Brightner.

'This is terrible,' Mr Penn said. 'What do we do now? Aggie's coming home this afternoon! She'll find her mother in a playpen. No, Pluck, a doctor can't help in a case like this. I think it just has to wear off... Come outside with me, then we can discuss it calmly.'

After they had gone out the front door and were standing on the walkway, Dolly flew up. 'I saw them!' she called.

'Who?'

'I saw Aggie. And the whole Stamper family. Mr Stamper and the six little Stampers! They're on the bus from Egham. On their way here! They'll be here in ten minutes.'

Mr Penn raced to the lift, dragging Pluck along behind him.

'Quick!' he called. 'We have to stop Aggie! She can't go home to her mother... that would be too much of a shock.'

Aggie Comes Home

Pluck and Mr Penn were standing on the pavement in front of the Pill Building. They were waiting for the bus from Egham. Aggie was on it with the whole Stamper family.

'Don't forget, Pluck,' Mr Penn said. 'No matter what, Aggie mustn't go up to her mother. We have to stop her. Imagine if she goes home... and finds her mother in the playpen. Crowing like a baby.'

'But how are we going to stop her?' Pluck asked. 'She'll be sure to want to go home. What do we say?'

But before Mr Penn could answer, there was a loud beeping and the bus pulled up. It stopped right in front of the entrance to the Pill Building and the door opened. Six little Stampers rolled out, screaming and shouting. Then Mr Stamper stepped off the bus with Aggie. They all had beautiful suntans. Aggie had gained some weight and she had a big smile on her face.

'Hello!' the little Stampers shouted. 'We're back!'

'You've been away for ages!' Pluck said.

'Six weeks,' Mr Stamper said. 'And the weather was beautiful the whole time! But we're still glad to be back home.'

'Me too,' Aggie said. 'I'm going straight up to see my mother.'

'Wait a second, Aggie,' Mr Penn said. 'Don't be in such a hurry... wait a second...'

Aggie looked a little surprised and asked, 'What do I have to wait for?'

'You can't go up to see your mother,' Mr Penn said nervously.

'What's wrong?' Aggie asked. 'Nothing's happened, has it? Is she sick?'

'Yes,' Mr Penn said. 'I'm afraid so.'

Now the Stampers started to get involved.

'Poor child!' Mr Stamper exclaimed. 'If your mother's sick, you can stay with us till she's better!'

'Come home with us!' the little Stampers shouted. 'It'll be fun!'

But Aggie wasn't listening. She slipped past Pluck and ran inside, into the lobby of the Pill Building.

'Stop her!' Mr Penn cried.

Pluck ran after Aggie but before he could catch her she stepped into the lift. And the lift doors closed right in front of Pluck's nose.

'Just what I was afraid of,' Mr Penn moaned. 'Now she's going to find her mother in the playpen!'

'What?' Mr Stamper said. 'What are you talking about?'

'We have to go after her... I'm not waiting for the lift... I'm going up the stairs,' Pluck cried. And he dashed up the stairs with all the little Stampers behind him.

They had to go to the nineteenth floor. And that meant climbing thirty-eight flights of stairs! And when they finally arrived, puffing and exhausted, they bumped into Mr Penn and Mr Stamper, who had taken the next lift.

On the way up, Mr Penn had told him what was happening, but Mr Stamper didn't really understand.

'She ate too much jam?' he said. 'But that won't turn you into a baby!'

'I'll explain later...' Mr Penn said. 'First we have to go and help Aggie... and comfort her... the poor child.'

They were now standing in front of Aggie's door and they rang the doorbell, because the door was locked. It took a very long time. Nobody came to the door.

Mr Penn groaned softly and kept muttering, 'Oh... the poor lamb... she must be paralysed with shock!'

But then the door opened and there was Aggie. Glowing and very happy.

'Come in, everyone,' she said. 'Then you can help with the drawing!'

They went inside. Mr Penn and Pluck and all the Stampers.

They followed Aggie to the living room.

And there was Mrs Brightner drawing on the freshly-painted walls.

'Hello,' she called. 'Come in. Grab a crayon and start drawing.'

The little Stampers cheered and rushed over to the box of crayons. They picked out the most beautiful colours and started drawing funny little men and women. Pluck joined in too, but Mr Stamper whispered to Mr Penn. 'She's not like a baby, more a little girl!'

'Yes,' Mr Penn whispered back. 'In one hour she's got a lot bigger. I mean... she's stopped being a baby and turned into a five-year-old... Remarkable!'

When all the walls had been covered with the craziest drawings, Mrs Brightner sat down with a smile on her face and called out, 'Phew, I'm exhausted! Who'd like a nice sandwich? I've made some delicious black-berry jam!'

'Hooray!' cried Aggie and all the little Stampers.

They were about to run into the kitchen to help, but Mr Penn yelled, 'Stop! Halt!'

Everyone fell silent with shock.

'Dear Mrs Brightner,' Mr Penn said solemnly. 'There's something I need to tell you. The jam you made is hasselberry jam. And hasselberries are delicious, but they are also dangerous when you eat too many of them.'

'Don't be silly!' Mrs Brightner laughed. 'I ate more than a pound of that jam and I've never felt better!'

'Exactly!' Mr Penn said. 'And tell me, Mrs Brightner, what did you do after you ate all that jam? Tell me exactly what you did.'

Mrs Brightner thought about it and shook her head vaguely. 'I don't remember...' she said. 'I only know that I saw some crayons and started drawing...'

'Do you know when you ate the jam?' Mr Penn asked. 'Was it yesterday? Or this morn-ing? Or an hour ago?'

Mrs Brightner rubbed her forehead with her hand and said, slightly confused, 'No – strange – I've forgotten... it's like I was un-conscious for a while...'

'That's exactly what I mean,' Mr Penn said. 'And that's why I would like to give you some good advice. Take a small mouthful of jam every day. A teaspoonful, no more. Keep the jam for yourself. Aggie doesn't need this kind of jam.'

'I'll take a small mouthful every day,' Mrs Brightner said. 'I promise. And now let's go and make lots of delicious things to eat.'

It turned into a fun party. They played all kinds of games together until everyone was exhausted and wanted to go home to bed. The Stampers went to their own flat, Mr Penn went to his shop and Pluck went up to his tower.

The next morning Aggie came to visit him.

'How's your mother?' Pluck asked.

'She's fantastic,' Aggie said. 'Pluck, she's changed so much. You know how she was always so strict? And so fussy? And everything always had to stay clean... and she never let me do anything. It's all changed. Now she plays with me.'

'Not the whole time?' Pluck asked. 'Not constantly?'

'No, she does ordinary things too, like the vacuuming and the dishes. But when she's finished, we play with the doll's house. Or we blow bubbles. And the living room looks lovely with all those drawings.'

'As long as she has her teaspoon of jam every day,' Pluck said. 'Then it will stay like that.'

'I'll make sure she never forgets,' Aggie said. 'But I'm a bit scared... What happens when the jam runs out?'

'There are fifty-four jars full of it,' Pluck said. 'Every day one little teaspoon... by the time the jam runs out, you'll be big.'

'Really?' Aggie said. 'So we don't need to worry about it now?'

'We don't need to worry about it now,' Pluck said.

The Curlicoo

Zaza the cockroach was not very talkative. Usually he just sat quietly in his corner gnawing on a piece of apple peel. But one day he said, 'Hey, Pluck, did anything ever come out of that egg?'

'What egg?' Pluck said.

'When you came back from Egham-on-Sea you had a big orange egg with you,' Zaza said. 'Remember?'

'Oh, yeah!' Pluck exclaimed. 'That's true. I forgot all about it. I gave it to Mr and Mrs Jeffrey to hatch. It's a good thing you mentioned it, Zaza. I'll go down right away and ask how it went.'

When Pluck rang the bell, Mrs Jeffrey opened the door. She turned very pale at the sight of Pluck standing there and immediately said, 'I know why you've come! You've come about the curlicoo.'

'I've come about the egg,' Pluck said.

'Yes,' she said. 'That's what I mean. We hatched it out in bed, remember? Under the electric blanket. It was a lot of bother because for weeks we had to sleep on one side of the bed to avoid breaking the egg. But finally a little chick hatched out. A curlicoo.'

'What's a curlicoo?' Pluck asked.

'A very strange bird,' Mrs Jeffrey said. 'It had hair instead of feathers. And it grew enormous. First we kept it in a cage, but it soon grew out of that. Then we let it loose in the living room, but it kept banging its head on the ceiling. And finally we let it out on the balcony. And we said, "Just fly away, dear, there's a good bird!"'

'And?' Pluck asked. 'Did it fly away?'

'If only it had,' Mrs Jeffrey said. 'It couldn't fly, you see. Maybe because it didn't have any feathers, just wispy, curly hair. We didn't know what kind of bird it was at that stage. But then one day a man came. He asked if he could see our strange bird. And immediately he said, "Oh, that's a curlicoo." And then he asked if he could have it. "I have a very large bird collection," he said.'

'And then?' Pluck asked.

Mrs Jeffrey was finding it hard to go on. She pulled out a hankie and sobbed.

'Tell me... what happened next?' Pluck asked.

'We thought...' Mrs Jeffrey said, choking... 'we thought our bird would like it there with all the other birds. And after a few days we went to see how it was settling in. And then...' She cried even louder.

Pluck waited patiently.

'And then we saw that it was a museum,' Mrs Jeffrey said. 'That man was the director of a museum. A bird museum. Full of stuffed birds.'

'Stuffed birds?' Pluck cried. 'You mean they were all dead? And the curlicoo's stuffed too?'

'Yes,' Mrs Jeffrey sighed. 'All the birds there are dead. And stuffed with straw. And they've got glass eyes. And we saw our very own curlicoo standing there... and then we left as fast as we could. That's all. We're so sorry we let that man take it, but he seemed so

respectable. He's called Mr Plomp and we're furious with him. But now it's too late.'

'Where is this museum?' Pluck asked. 'I'll go have a look.'

'On Market Square,' said Mrs Jeffrey. 'Oh, Pluck... it was such a sweet thing... it didn't sing, but it always called, "Prrr... ta-lee-loo!" Such a lovely sound. And now it's dead.'

Pluck said goodbye and drove to Market Square. A sign on a beautiful, big old house said: BIRD MUSEUM.

Inside it was dark and silent. There was a musty smell. A man in a white coat was sitting in a glass office. He was probably the director, Mr Plomp. Pluck went into the display room.

Everywhere there were stuffed birds in glass cases: stiff and rigid, with glass eyes. There were bird skeletons here and there too. And in a back corner there was an enormous cage. And in that cage there was a very large bird. And on the cage there was a sign saying: CURLICOO.

Pluck looked at it very carefully. 'That's so horrible...' he mumbled. 'Killing a beautiful animal just to stuff it. And giving it glass eyes.' He stared at the curlicoo's eyes. And to Pluck's astonishment he saw that they weren't made of glass at all. There was a glint in those eyes and they were looking at him. They were alive.

170

'Pssst...' Pluck said. 'I don't think you're the least bit dead.'

The curlicoo didn't make a sound and it didn't move either. It stood there as motionless as the other birds, but its sad eyes were still looking at Pluck.

'Poor curlicoo,' Pluck said. 'Shall we come and rescue you? I've got lots of friends... just be patient... we'll come and get you.'

Now the bird moved. It shook its wings, opened its beak and called, 'Prrr... ta-lee-loo!'

The sound boomed through the museum. Pluck was terribly shocked and stepped back into a dark corner, because the director had come out of his office and was running up. He had an assistant with him, also wearing a white coat.

'Mr Peterson!' the director snapped. 'Haven't you stuffed the curlicoo yet? You heard it, the beast screeches! We can't have that here. Why isn't it stuffed?'

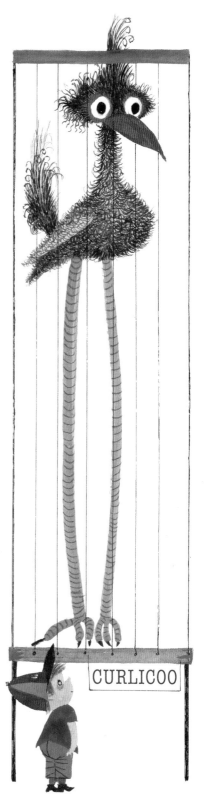

CURLICOO

'I was going to do it this morning,' the other man said. 'But I was so awfully busy. And I thought, *The creature hardly moves, nobody will notice it's still alive.*'

'Then do it at once,' the director said. 'Make sure of it, Mr Peterson.'

'Very good, Mr Plomp,' Mr Peterson said. 'I'll do it first thing tomorrow morning. I'll have time then.'

They went back to their office and Pluck emerged from the corner where he had been hiding. He didn't dare say another word to the poor curlicoo. He was afraid it might call again. Quickly he slipped out of the building, climbed into his truck and drove off.

Bright red with indignation, he reached Mr Penn's bookshop.

When he had told the whole story, Mr Penn said, 'You're right, we have to do something.'

'And as quickly as possible!' Pluck cried. 'Let's break in there tonight!'

'But what if they stuff the curlicoo today?' Mr Penn said. 'We'll be too late. Let me think for a moment.'

Mr Penn closed his eyes and thought about it. Finally he said, 'I've got an idea. Do you think the Stampers will help?'

'Of course!' Pluck cried.

'And Aggie too?'

'I'm sure of it!'

'I need a van,' Mr Penn said. 'I'll ask the florist next door... They won't mind me borrowing their van for an hour.'

'What are we going to do?' Pluck asked impatiently.

'I need a wig too,' Mr Penn said. 'And a moustache. And big sunglasses. Come with me, Pluck, we've got work to do.'

'But *what* are we going to do?' Pluck insisted.

'You'll see,' said Mr Penn.

A Trick

The bird museum was on Market Square. It was full of stuffed birds, but there was one bird that was still alive. The curlicoo. But it wouldn't be alive for long... soon they were going to stuff it.

There were cars parked in front of the museum. Rows and rows of cars. In the middle there was also a van from a florist's.

A man went into the museum. He was clearly a photographer. He had long hair, a big moustache and enormous sunglasses. Camera in hand, he knocked on the glass door of the director's office.

'Hello, Mr Plomp,' the photographer said. 'I'm from the *Full-Colour Ladies' Magazine*. That's a weekly, you know. I'd like to take a few photos.'

'Excellent,' Mr Plomp said. 'I have some magnificent stuffed birds. Go ahead!'

'We've heard that you have a real curlicoo,' the photographer said. 'May I take a picture of it?'

'Of course, come this way.'

Mr Plomp led the photographer to the tall cage.

'Oh, this bird has been beautifully stuffed,' the photographer said. 'It looks like it's still alive.'

'It is alive,' the director said. 'It should have been stuffed ages ago, but, well... no time... We're short-staffed.'

'If you could stand next to the cage,' the photographer said, 'I'll take a photo of you and the bird together.

'My pleasure!' the director said, going over to stand next to the cage.

'Oh, it's rather dark in here!' the photographer exclaimed. 'We should do this outside. You and the curlicoo in front of the museum.'

'Um...' Mr Plomp said hesitantly. 'A bit difficult... a bit of a chore moving the cage, you see.'

'What if we put the bird on the pavement without a cage... will it fly away?'

'No, not at all. Curlicoos can't fly. But it can walk —'

'We'll make sure it doesn't run off,' the photographer said.

The director opened the cage. The poor curlicoo looked scared and stood there as stiff as a board. They had to carry it out.

And now it was standing on the pavement next to Mr Plomp.

'Magnificent!' the photographer cried. 'Just hold that for a second! What wonderful light. What beautiful colours!'

A group of children had stopped to watch. If you looked closely, you would have seen that it was the Stampers... with Pluck between them and Aggie a little further along. But it looked like they just happened to be passing by.

'There!' the photographer exclaimed cheerfully. 'This will be a fantastic shot. And now I would very much like to take a photo of you by yourself, Mr Plomp. After all, you're very well known, famous even! If you just go

and stand over there. And then look up for a moment.'

Mr Plomp went over to stand where the photographer wanted him. He looked up obediently.

'Smile now!' the photographer called. 'That's right... yes... hold that... I'll make a whole series of photos! You're going to be in the *Full-Colour Ladies' Weekly*!'

The director stood there patiently smiling until the photographer took his last snap and said, 'Thank you very much, Mr Plomp.'

But in that same instant all of the children started screaming and yelling.

Mr Plomp spun around. The curlicoo was gone. The pavement was empty. 'There! It went down there, down that lane!' a little boy screamed, pointing with one finger.

'Yes, we saw it run off... into that lane!' all the other children shouted. They all pointed in the same direction.

Mr Plomp didn't hesitate. He stormed over the pavement, wriggled through between the parked cars and ran into the lane. There were cars and trucks parked here too. He tripped over a rubbish bin and fell, *wham*... flat on his face on some mucky pear peel.

Mr Plomp groaned, then got up and ran. As he trotted along, he asked everyone he met, 'Did you see a bird walk past? Did a bird go into any of these houses? Did you see a big bird around here anywhere?'

The people looked surprised and shook their heads. And the curlicoo was nowhere to be seen.

Mr Plomp rang doorbells here and there, but no one had seen the curlicoo, and in the end he went back to the museum in despair.

The photographer had disappeared. And the children were gone too. The florist's van wasn't there anymore either, but Mr Plomp didn't notice that. He ran into the museum and sat down panting at his desk to ring the police.

'A bird has run away?' the policeman on the other end of the line asked.

'A rare curlicoo!' Mr Plomp shouted. 'It ran off!'

By this time the van was miles away. Mr Stamper was at the wheel and Pluck and the photographer were in the back with the curlicoo. The poor creature was all folded up. The photographer took off his wig. He ripped the moustache off his face and said, 'Well? Did we bring that off nicely or didn't we?'

'Fantastic, Mr Penn,' said Pluck.

In front of the Pill Building they stopped to wait for the little Stampers and Aggie, who had walked all the way back from the museum.

'Here they come!' Pluck said.

Cheering, the whole troop of them came running up.

'It went great, didn't it?' the little Stampers shouted.

'He didn't suspect a thing!' Aggie laughed.

'Shhhh...' Mr Penn said. 'Not so loud... people might hear. And now we have to discuss things. What do we do with the curlicoo?'

'Our house!' the Stampers shouted.

'No,' Mr Penn said. 'That's too dangerous. People would hear it call! I think for now we'd better hide it in the storeroom at the back of my shop. Nobody will see it there and nobody will hear it.'

'Why don't we just let it go?' Mr Stamper asked. 'It can fly away.'

'The poor creature can't fly, that's the problem. And if we just let it go, it will walk off and get caught and taken back to the museum.'

'We'll pick it up and carry it inside,' Pluck said. 'But we'll have to wait till no one's around.'

It took a very long time for the right moment to arrive. People kept passing by on the pavement and Pluck was terrified they would see the crest and feet of the folded-up curlicoo sticking out of the van. But fortunately they all hurried by without looking and finally Mr Penn called out, 'Yes! Now!'

As fast as lightning, the six little Stampers pulled the bird out of the back of the van and carried it into the shop. Not a soul saw them.

They put it down in the back of the storeroom with a bowl of feed and a bowl of water.

Later that day, when Pluck turned on the radio, he heard a police report: *A so-called curlicoo has escaped from the bird museum. This animal has hair instead of feathers. Its call is 'Prrr... ta-lee-loo'! There is a large reward for whoever returns the bird...*

'Oh, no!' Pluck said to Zaza the cockroach. 'Did you hear that?'

'I heard it all right,' said Zaza. 'If I were you, I'd move that animal somewhere far-away where there's no houses or people. It's bound to be discovered!'

'Aren't you gloomy again,' Pluck said. But he wasn't feeling very relaxed about it either.

Prrr... Ta-lee-loo

The curlicoo was in Mr Penn's storeroom. Now and then it let out a shrill cry. As long as the door was shut properly, nobody heard it. So they made sure the door was shut tight.

A small girl came into the shop.

It was Lisa-Beth, who had come to buy a box of crayons. And just when she had paid and was leaving the shop, Pluck came out of the storeroom where he had fed the curlicoo. The door was open for a split second and in that split second the curlicoo called, 'Prrr... ta-lee-loo!'

Pluck closed the door quickly behind him. Lisa-Beth had left the shop, but Mr Penn snapped, 'That wasn't very clever of you, Pluck! You should have listened first to make sure no one was in the shop. That child must have heard.'

'No, it wasn't clever of me...' Pluck said, 'but she's such a little girl, I'm sure she didn't notice. I wish the curlicoo would just keep its beak shut! I keep telling it, "Be quiet!" But it's so glad we rescued it from the museum it won't stop calling.'

'Next thing that child will report us,' Mr Penn said. 'And then the police will come to search the premises and then what? This is all too risky. But I do have an idea.'

Mr Penn pulled out a machine.

'A tape recorder?' Pluck said. 'What are you going to do with that?'

'You'll find out,' Mr Penn said. 'Go outside and see if Dolly the pigeon is around. And Carl the seagull too, if possible.'

Pluck went outside. He found Dolly soon enough but Carl was nowhere in sight.

'I'll get him,' Dolly said.

She flew off and came back ten minutes later with Carl, the seagull with the wooden leg.

'Ahoy,' Carl called. 'Is something exciting going on?'

'Mr Penn wants to see you,' Pluck said.

'Both of you.' And he opened the shop door for them. He didn't go back inside himself, but walked along the pavement, where Lisa-Beth came up holding a doll.

'That's a pretty doll you've got there,' Pluck said.

'I'm going to get a much prettier one,' Lisa-Beth said. 'As soon as my mother gets the money for the bird.'

Pluck turned pale with fright. 'What do you mean?' he said. 'Which bird?'

'A bird escaped,' said Lisa-Beth. 'And the person who finds it gets lots of money. And I know where it is. There!' And she pointed at Mr Penn's shop.

'Don't be silly,' Pluck said. 'There aren't any birds in the bookshop.'

'Yes, there is,' Lisa-Beth said. 'I heard it. It goes "Prrr... ta-lee-loo." I went and told my mother straightaway. And my mother called the police. And soon the police will be here to search the bookshop!'

Pluck almost shouted, 'You nasty little sneak!' But he kept a grip on himself. And after Lisa-Beth had skipped off with her doll, he slipped in to Mr Penn's and said, 'We've been betrayed! The police are coming!'

'Just as I thought!' Mr Penn cried. 'That child, no doubt!'

'You have to go, quick!' he said to Dolly and Carl. 'And thanks for your help.'

The birds flew off and Mr Penn grabbed a roll of sticky tape and dragged Pluck into the storeroom.

'Tape up its beak,' Mr Penn said. 'Quick.'

Pluck wrapped the tape around and around the curlicoo's beak so it couldn't make any more noise.

Then Mr Penn picked up the bird and put it in a kind of gap between two dark book-cases.

'Give me those two big posters,' he said to Pluck.

Pluck held them out. They were enormously large posters. Mr Penn hung them up one above the other, just in front of the curlicoo, so that the bird was completely hidden behind them.

You couldn't see anything of it at all. Only two big feet sticking out at the bottom.

'We'll have to think of something for that,' Mr Penn mumbled.

Just then they heard the shop door open.

Mr Penn walked into the shop calmly. A policeman was standing there.

'Are you Mr Penn?' he asked. 'We have received information that the escaped curlicoo is located in this location.'

'Here?' Mr Penn said with surprise. 'In this shop? Well, you can see that it isn't. How did anyone get that idea?'

'They heard its call,' the policeman said. 'The creature has a rather special call to it, you know. It sounds something like "Prrr... ta-lee-loo". A little girl heard it here. And therefore I would like to take a look in the back of your shop.'

'Go ahead,' Mr Penn said, smiling. 'But that girl only heard a tape.'

'What do you mean?'

'An audiotape,' Mr Penn said. 'You see, I collect birdcalls. I record all kinds of noises made by birds. Here, with this tape recorder. Would you like to hear them?'

He turned it on. The reels started turning. And there it was, 'Ahoy... eeeee... eeeee...' the shrill screech of a seagull.

'That was a seagull,' Mr Penn said. 'Keep listening.'

'Coo... coo...'

'A pigeon,' the policeman said, moved.

'Exactly,' said Mr Penn. 'And now, listen closely!'

'Prrr... ta-lee-loo!' echoed through the shop. 'See?' Mr Penn said in a friendly voice. 'That's what the girl heard.'

'Yes, but...' the policeman said, 'where did you record that? You must have had the bird here!'

'It was in the museum!' Mr Penn said. 'I went there last week. You see, I thought, *Ah, a bird museum! I can record lots of bird noises.* But unfortunately, all of the birds were stuffed, and stuffed birds don't make a sound, as you know. Only this one bird was still alive. And that was how I was able to record it on this tape.'

'Ah, that explains it,' said the policeman. 'This tape was all the young lady heard.'

'Just this tape,' said Mr Penn.

'Still, I must look out the back anyway,' the policeman said. 'It's my duty.'

'Go ahead,' said Mr Penn, opening the storeroom door.

Pluck was sitting writing at a table just in front of the giant posters. The policeman looked around. Very briefly.

Then he said, 'That's all in order, sir. Sorry to disturb you.'

'Not at all,' Mr Penn said and he showed the policeman out.

'What a brilliant idea!' Pluck cried, emerging from the storeroom. 'You recorded Carl's and Dolly's voices, and then the call of the curlicoo!'

'Yes,' Mr Penn said. 'And it all sounded very plausible, didn't it? But now I'm too scared to keep the curlicoo here any longer. We need to take it somewhere else, somewhere safe… somewhere nobody will hear it. Think of somewhere, Pluck.'

'What about Dovey Gardens?' Pluck asked hesitantly.

'That's not a bad idea at all,' Mr Penn said. 'Dovey Gardens is a long way away, right at the far end of the park. Tonight, when it's dark, we'll take the curlicoo there.'

I'm an Extinct Bird

Pluck was at home in his room in the tower. He was eating a chocolate-spread sandwich while Zaza the cockroach, who was sitting next to him on the tablecloth, kept nagging. 'Tell me more, Pluck, tell me more…'

'You want me to tell you more about the curlicoo?' Pluck asked. 'But there's nothing more to tell. It's in Dovey Gardens. We took it there last night. And now the heron's giving it flying lessons.'

'And what if someone spots it?' Zaza asked. 'If kids go to play in Dovey Gardens, kids we don't know? And they see it? Or hear it?'

'It promised to keep its beak shut,' Pluck said. 'We said, "Remember, if you so much as squeak, we'll tape up your beak again." And then it went very quiet. Because it hated that tape.'

Someone rapped hard on the window.

'It's Carl the seagull!' Zaza cried. 'Hide me, Pluck, quick! He's scary.'

Pluck put the cheese cover over Zaza and let Carl with the wooden leg in.

'Ahoy,' said Carl. 'You have to come and help, Pluck. The flying lessons aren't going well.'

'Isn't the curlicoo a good learner?' Pluck asked.

'I don't think he wants to learn,' Carl said. 'He stands on a hill and the heron shows him how to fly. And all the birds stand around and everyone shouts, "Do your best, Curlicoo!" And you know what he says?'

Pluck shrugged.

'He says, "If I could fly, where would I fly to?"'

'But he could just fly away,' Pluck said.

'That's what we keep saying. "Don't be silly," we shout. "As soon as you can fly, just fly away." But then he says, "Which way?" And then we say, "Away from here." And then he says, "Which way from here?"'

'You won't get very far that way,' Pluck sighed.

'That's just it,' Carl said. 'You know what I think? The curlicoo was in the bird museum. And next to his cage there was a sign that said: Extinct Bird. And the director of the bird museum kept saying it too: "The curlicoos have all died out. The curlicoo is an extinct bird." Do you understand, Pluck? The curlicoo started to believe it. Now he keeps saying, "I'm an extinct bird."'

'He can't be extinct,' Pluck said. 'He's alive.'

'That's what we keep telling him. "You're not extinct," we say. "You're alive." But he says, "I am extinct, because there are no other curlicoos anywhere in the whole wide world."'

'Is it possible?' Pluck asked. 'Have all the other curlicoos all over the world died out? Is our curlicoo the very last one?'

'I don't believe a word of it,' Carl said. 'The curlicoo came out of an egg, didn't he? Then he must have had a mother and a father, just like everyone else. And brothers and sisters too, probably. I've got an idea, Pluck. Let me out.'

Pluck rushed over to open the window, but quickly asked, 'What's your idea, Carl? Where are you going in such a hurry?'

'I might be gone for a long time,' Carl said. 'I'm going to search for the other curlicoos. I'm going on a very long trip, Pluck! Ahoy!'

And with a loud screech, Carl flew out of the window.

Pluck released Zaza from his prison.

'I'm glad he's gone,' Zaza said. 'I'm so scared of him. He always gives me such a hungry look. Give me an apple peel to get over the fright, Pluck.'

'Here,' Pluck said. 'And now I have to go. I'm going to see how the curlicoo is getting on.'

He drove his tow truck to Dovey Gardens and in the park he saw Dolly coming to meet him. And Dolly told him exactly the same story all over again. The flying lessons weren't going well. 'I think it's because curlicoos have hair instead of feathers,' Dolly said. 'How can you fly without feathers?'

'I'll come and have a look,' Pluck said.

He saw the poor curlicoo on top of a hill in Dovey Gardens with lots of birds around him. The heron kept showing him how to fly, but all the curlicoo did was flap his wings a little.

'Shall I put him up in the tree?' Pluck asked. 'With my crane? Then he'll have to fly.'

It wasn't easy winching the curlicoo up and putting him down on a branch of the oak tree. But when they had finally managed and the poor terrified creature was standing there trembling on a branch, the heron shouted out in a very strict voice, 'Now jump. Go!'

'You can do it!' Pluck called. 'Come on!'

The curlicoo stood up straight, flapped his big hairy wings and cried very loudly, 'Prrr... ta-lee-loo!'

Then there was a fluttering noise and a dull thud. He'd dropped like a bag of cement.

Pluck helped him back up onto his feet. Fortunately he hadn't hurt himself.

'You promised not to make any noise,'

Pluck said firmly. 'And now you've gone and called again! That wasn't very clever of you. You have to keep your beak shut. Come on, we'll try again.'

They winched the curlicoo back up into the tree. Even more birds had arrived to watch. And not just birds. The other animals from Dovey Gardens were standing around too. And because they were all watching so intently, none of them noticed the little girl peering at them from behind a bush. It was Lisa-Beth. She had seen Pluck driving to Dovey Gardens in his tow truck and had sneaked along behind him. She'd lost him for a moment, because Dovey Gardens was big and full of winding paths, and she'd even been scared she might not be able to find her way home. But then, all of a sudden, she heard the call of the curlicoo.

Now she was standing close-by and spying on them and she saw the curlicoo fall out of the tree a second time. And while all the birds chirped and chattered excitedly, Lisa-Beth crept off away from Dovey Gardens.

'The nincompoop's not trying!' the heron shouted angrily. 'He can do it, he just doesn't want to!'

'Shall we try one last time?' Pluck asked.

But the curlicoo looked at him sadly and said, 'Forget it. I'm just an extinct bird anyway.'

'I think I'll go and talk to Mr Penn,' Pluck said. 'Have a little rest. I'll be back soon.'

He drove off through the park to Mr Penn's shop. But the little girl Lisa-Beth was nowhere to be seen along the way. She was already back home, telling her mother what she'd seen and heard.

Lisa-Beth

Mr Plomp, the director of the bird museum, was on the phone shouting excitedly. 'What's that? Your daughter has seen the curlicoo? Where?'

Lisa-Beth's mother was on the other end of the line. 'The curlicoo is in Dovey Gardens,' she said.

'Where's that?' Mr Plomp asked.

'My daughter will show you. Just go to the park. She's waiting for you there.'

'We're on our way!' Mr Plomp said in a grim voice. He called his assistant and said,

'Mr Peterson, the curlicoo has been located. Get the big net. We'll take the jeep.'

In Dovey Gardens, the curlicoo was standing on the hill and trying to fly. The heron kept patiently demonstrating how, but it all came to nothing. The curlicoo just couldn't do it. And every time he failed, he said despondently, 'What good is it? If I could fly, where would I fly to?'

This made the other birds angry and impatient. 'Away!' they called. 'Just fly away!'

Meanwhile Pluck was in Mr Penn's shop discussing it all. 'We have to take the curlicoo somewhere safer,' he said. 'It's too dangerous in Dovey Gardens. Sooner or later kids are going to hear him call. What if that nasty Lisa-Beth heard him? She knows there's a big reward for finding the curlicoo.'

'You're right, we have to get him out of there,' Mr Penn said. 'We'll take him to the countryside... tonight, when it's dark. Somewhere where there aren't any people or houses.'

'He'll get lonely,' Pluck said. 'And how will he find food and –' He didn't finish his sentence, because Dolly flew in, shouting excitedly, 'Come quick! We've been betrayed! They're on their way to Dovey Gardens.'

'Who?' Mr Penn cried.

'The men from the museum and that little brat, Lisa-Beth! In a jeep!'

Pluck was already out the door and in his tow truck. He drove faster than ever. In a flash he was at the pond... too late!

The jeep was already leaving Dovey Gardens. The museum director and his assistant were in the front. And lying in the back was the poor curlicoo, wrapped in a net with Lisa-Beth on the seat in front of him. She looked very prissy and very proud of herself, and she pretended not to notice Pluck.

Bright red with anger, Pluck bit back a very nasty word. He did a U-turn and followed the jeep through the back streets to the museum. When they got there the jeep drove in through a big gate. And when Pluck got out of his truck, the museum doorman slammed the gate shut in his face.

'Let me in!' Pluck shouted.

'The museum's closed,' the doorman said. 'It's Monday. On Monday we're closed. We're too busy stuffing birds.'

Pluck groaned. Now they had the poor curlicoo in their clutches. And they were going to kill him. And stuff him. And there was nothing Pluck could do.

Then he felt something land on his shoulder. It was Dolly the pigeon.

'What can we do, Dolly?' Pluck sobbed. 'Where are they?'

'They're in the museum courtyard,' Dolly said. 'I just flew over it. I saw the poor curlicoo standing there with those two murderers next to him.'

'You mean they're outside?' Pluck asked.

'Yes, the courtyard's open,' Dolly said. 'There's no roof. If the curlicoo could fly, he could escape easily.'

The gate opened and Lisa-Beth came out. With a big lollipop. They'd given her that as a thank-you. But the big reward was still to come, that was what Mr Plomp said. Her mother would get the reward tomorrow.

Pluck glared at her silently as she walked past. She blushed and suddenly ran off as if she was scared of him.

'Fly over the courtyard again,' Pluck said. 'Have another look...'

'I'm too scared,' Dolly said. 'It's too horrible. Oh, Pluck... maybe he's already dead...'

But the curlicoo wasn't dead yet. He was standing in the dark museum courtyard. Bent over and miserable, with his beak bent and his hair messed up. The director was standing next to him. He pulled the net off the bird.

'Careful,' the assistant said. 'Otherwise it will fly off after all.'

'It can't fly,' Mr Plomp said. 'The stupid thing! Huh? Hey, curlicoo? You're nice and flightless, aren't you?'

The curlicoo shrunk even more and shivered.

'So,' the director said. 'Now we need to stuff this beautiful specimen as fast as we can. Get the equipment, Mr Peterson.'

Mr Peterson trotted into the museum, returning with a couple of bottles and a big needle.

'I'll hold it,' Mr Plomp said. But when he grabbed the curlicoo by the neck, there was a rough, loud screech over the courtyard, 'Ahoy!'

'Chase that seagull away!' the director shouted. 'It's getting in our way. Ow!'

Carl had slapped him in the face with a wing. And Carl's wings were strong and hard.

Mr Plomp swung his arms at Carl. 'Go away, bird!' he shouted. 'Or we'll stuff you too.' He tried to grab the curlicoo again, while Mr Peterson came closer with the needle, but Carl screeched menacingly and lashed out hard with both wings, driving the men back.

'Listen...' Carl shouted to the curlicoo. 'Listen. I found them! The other curlicoos! You're not alone! You're not extinct! Your father and your mother are there... on the Isle of Eem, far out to sea!'

'Chase that seagull away! And grab the curlicoo!' Mr Plomp screamed.

Mr Peterson lunged at Carl again, but he got such a hard whack in return that he screamed with pain.

'Come with me, come with me...' Carl cried. 'Overseas... overseas... to the Isle of Eem, where the curlicoos live... your brothers and sisters... your whole family... come with me!'

'I'll get you, you horrible creature!' Mr Plomp shouted, reaching for the curlicoo with both arms. But just when he was about to grab him, the curlicoo stepped aside. He flapped his wings and took off. For a moment, he looked like he was going to sink down again, but then Carl called out one more time, 'Come with me...' and the curlicoo took off. Like a heron, calmly flapping his wings. He did one little circle over the heads of the astonished men.

'Look over there!' Dolly cried on the other side of the gate.

Pluck looked up.

'Prrr... ta-lee-loo!' sounded over his head... and, 'Ahoy!'

Pluck did a crazy little jig. 'He can fly!' he shouted. 'I know what happened. Carl found the other curlicoos. Now our curlicoo finally knows where to fly to!'

There were two other people who saw the curlicoo flying overhead. Lisa-Beth and her mother. 'There goes our reward,' her mother said furiously. 'It's flying away!'

Goodbye!

Pluck woke up very early in the morning and thought, *What is it today? Oh, yeah! It's my birthday! And nobody knows because I haven't told them. It's going to be a really boring day...*

Feeling a little sad, he got up and had a wash. Then he looked around. Where was Zaza the cockroach? He wasn't in his corner. And he wasn't in the cupboard either. Zaza was nowhere to be found.

'Where are you? Where have you got to?' Pluck called anxiously.

Then he heard a very small, scared voice, 'Help!'

It was coming from the table. Yesterday Pluck had left the jam jar open.

'Good grief, you're in the jam!' Pluck exclaimed with fright. 'Hang on!'

He lowered a spoon into the jar and Zaza dragged himself up out of the jam.

'Zaza, that was stupid, you could have sunk into it and choked to death,' Pluck said. 'And look at you! You're all sticky. I'll hold you under the tap.'

'No!' Zaza cried. 'Cockroaches die under the tap.'

'Then I'll wipe you off with a cloth.' When he looked reasonably clean again, Zaza said, 'Many happy returns.'

'Oh, you know it's my birthday!' Pluck exclaimed happily. 'That's nice. Thank you.'

'I had such a great idea,' said Zaza. 'To decorate the table. First I was going to walk through the jam, and then over the tablecloth. Round and round in circles making pretty red shapes... but I sunk into the jam'

'I think it's a very sweet idea,' Pluck said. 'But never do it again! Here's a bit of apple peel.'

They started to eat breakfast together and Pluck kept thinking, *What a boring birthday this will be... nobody even knows about it.*

Then something flew against the window with a thud. It was Carl with the wooden leg.

Pluck quickly put the cheese cover over Zaza and opened the window.

Carl flew in and laid a dead fish on Pluck's sandwich.

'Here!' he said. 'Happy birthday.'

'Oh... thank you...' Pluck stammered, blushing. 'How did you know it was my birthday?'

'I heard,' Carl said. 'Eat it up straightaway! It's fresh from the sea!'

'I, um... I'd rather eat it this evening,' Pluck said. 'But tell me, how's the curlicoo.'

'Excellent,' Carl said. 'He's on the Isle of Eem with the other curlicoos. His father and mother and lots of sisters... He said to say hello. Well, I'll be off then. Have a good birthday. Ahoy!' And Carl flew off.

Pluck let Zaza out again. And now someone else came in through the window. It was Dolly the pigeon. She had a letter in her beak but before sitting down she quickly flew over the tablecloth.

'Hey!' Pluck screamed. 'Dolly, what are you doing? You did something on my table. That's disgusting.'

'Best wishes for your birthday,' Dolly said politely. 'And you're an ungrateful boy. Because what I do is good luck! And you should know that. And this letter's from your friends. Open it.'

Pluck opened the letter. It said:

Dear Pluck, it's your birthday. But your room in the tower is a little small for all of us. Come down to the street instead.

Pluck blushed. 'Who's down on the street?' he asked.

'Come and see for yourself,' Dolly said. And she flew out of the window.

'I have to go downstairs, Zaza,' Pluck said. 'Would you like to come with me? In a box?'

'No, I always prefer to stay home,' Zaza said. 'But I'll wait for you.'

Pluck took the lift downstairs. After he'd gone through the door and was out on the street, he saw his own little tow truck, all decorated with flags and flowers. Mr Penn was sitting in it. And so was Aggie. Behind it was the Stamper family's old car with Mr Stamper and the six little Stampers sitting in it. Everyone started cheering when Pluck came outside. And they sang, *Happy birthday to Pluck!*

'Thank you...' Pluck mumbled. They all gave him presents and he sat down on the pavement to unwrap them. Comics, a cowboy belt, coloured pencils and a very small camera. And lots more.

Pluck kept on saying, 'How did you know it was my birthday? I didn't think anyone knew.'

But everyone just laughed. And then Mr Stamper said, 'We had an idea. We thought we could all go for a long drive together. Our car is working again now. We could both drive... What do you say?'

'Great,' said Pluck. 'Where shall we go?'

'You decide,' said Mr Penn. 'It's your birthday. You tell us.' Pluck thought for a moment. And the others waited for him to think of something.

And in the silence, Pluck suddenly heard a quiet sound in his pocket, *'Toooo-toooo.'*

The Tootenlisp. Quickly Pluck pulled out the beautiful pink shell and held it up to his ear. 'To the Hathe...' said the Tootenlisp's tiny voice.

'To the what?'

'The Hathe.'

'Oh, I know where you mean! The River Haze! You want us to visit the tell me where-wolf, don't you?'

'That would be nithe,' said the Tootenlisp.

'Then we'll do it.'

'And all the betht for your birthday,'

rustled the shell. Then it fell silent again.

Pluck slipped it into his pocket and said, 'I know where to go. I promised the ferryman who runs the small ferry over the Haze that I'd come back. It's a fun drive.'

'Then we'll do that!' the whole gang yelled.

The Stampers went in their old car and Pluck went in the tow truck with Aggie and Mr Penn.

'We can put the presents in my shop for now,' Mr Penn said.

When they were finally about to drive off, an old friend of Pluck's came by. It was the Major on Longmount. He gave Pluck a present. A drum with drumsticks. 'Have a good trip! And come back soon!' the Major called.

'There's my mother...' Aggie cried. And she was right. Mrs Brightner came running up, puffing and panting. She gave Pluck a picture she had painted herself. Because fortunately Mrs Brightner still liked to draw and play games. She ate a teaspoon of hasselberry jam every day and that was a great help.

'Goodbye!' she called. 'Take care and have a good trip!'

'Thank you,' Pluck said.

And then they drove off in the old car and the little red tow truck.

All the people who lived in the Pill Building were standing on their balconies waving.

'Bye, Pluck!' they called. 'Come back soon!'

Then they turned the corner. Heading south.

And flying above them were Dolly and Carl.

Annie M.G. Schmidt

Annie M.G. Schmidt was born on 20th May 1911 in Zeeland, the Netherlands. After high school she trained as a librarian and worked in the Amsterdam children's library. Later she became head librarian of the public library in the city of Vlissingen. After the Second World War, she got a job with the Amsterdam newspaper *Het Parool*. She wrote pieces for adults and poems for children and the way she did it was very unusual for the time: not posh or fancy, but down-to-earth. Annie M.G. Schmidt was soon famous.

Her collaboration with illustrator Fiep Westendorp became legendary. It started with *Jip and Janneke, Tow-Truck Pluck, Otje* and *Scrumple*. She also had great success with other titles including *The Cat Who Came in off the Roof*, available from Pushkin Children's Books.

Annie M.G. Schmidt wrote for radio and TV too – songs, musicals and radio plays – but she was most famous for her children's books. In 1988 Astrid Lindgren presented her with the biggest prize that exists for children's books, the Hans Christian Andersen Award.

Annie M.G. Schmidt died on 21st May 1995 in Amsterdam.

Fiep Westendorp

Fiep Westendorp was born on 17th December 1916 in Zaltbommel, the Netherlands. After finishing high school, she attended the School of Applied Art in 's-Hertogenbosch, before going on to the Rotterdam Art Academy. Once qualified, she did book illustration, cover illustrations and drawings for advertisements.

After the Second World War, she went to work for the newspaper *Het Parool*, where she met Annie M.G. Schmidt. In 1952, the first *Jip and Janneke* adventure appeared on the newspaper's children's page. It was the start of a long and fruitful collaboration.

Fiep Westendorp did thousands of drawings, but her most famous work was her illustrations for the children's stories and poetry of Annie M.G. Schmidt, Mies Bouhouys and Han G. Hoekstra. In 1997, she received a major award that was created specially to honour her body of work, the Oeuvre Paintbrush.

Fiep Westendorp died on 3rd February 2004 in Amsterdam.